Winding Roads

A Bournemouth Writing Prize Anthology

Foreword

Journeys. We are all on one.

Whether it is walking down a gravel path, listening to the stone crunch beneath our feet or gazing up at the sky, wondering if there is a bigger purpose out there, journeys allow us to grow in different ways, encountering new experiences that lead us to that treasured final destination.

Sometimes when travelling, we can't see any progress, dread or fear can reduce our determination and slow us down but – if we are lucky - someone will offer encouragement, be a guide or boost our motivation to proceed. This anthology has been cultivated to act like that person - travelling down the same road and keeping you on track with tales of journeys in far off places.

As the editing team of Winding Roads, we selected these poems and stories from submissions to The Bournemouth Writing Prize 2021, each with their own unique style and voice. We hope you enjoy your travels with them as much as we have.

Emily, Lizzie, Daniella, Sriyanka (Editors)

The Bournemouth Writing Prize is run annually by Fresher Publishing at Bournemouth University, and this anthology was created by students of BU's MA Creative Writing & Publishing.

www.fresherpublishing.co.uk

Table Of Contents

Nearly Tall

Anita Lawrence

'Nearly Tall' was inspired by a WhatsApp writing challenge entitled 'Growing Down', devised to create and share art during Lockdown. The poem popped into Anita's consciousness early one morning, and she jotted it down even before she was fully awake.

Growing from tiny to small
Then shooting up to nearly tall
Clothes tighten
Loose shoes a squeeze
Big bikes and swings shrink so fast I bump my knees!
Huge steps and trees suddenly small
Each stretch and climb no effort or fall
But I haven't grown to nearly tall
The world simply grew down and that is all

Becoming Sarah Bernhardt

Emma Latham

Emma is a Devon-based writer and theatre maker. Emma trained with the Theatre Royal Plymouth's LAB Company and is currently studying for an MSt in Creative Writing at the University of Oxford. She was the writer-in-residence at Marlborough Primary School for the With Flying Colours Project. Her writing has been performed at RADA, Theatre 503, The Brockley Jack and the LAB Theatre Royal Plymouth.

All I wanted was to be like Sarah Bernhardt. At the age of 14,whilst being dragged around yet another car boot sale, I found an old postcard of her pretending to be dead and I thought, that's a woman to look up to. I knew at once she was everything I wanted to be; artistic, avantgarde and undeniably sexy. I decided to try and emulate her in every way I could. To be honest, becoming a world famous actress seemed less important than being morbid and glamourous and taking as many lovers as possible. However, when the teacher announced in assembly that they would be holding auditions for Hamlet, I knew that destiny was calling.

Sarah Bernhardt had played Hamlet loads of times; a woman could play male roles back then, a bit like in panto. So I curled my hair, bought an armful of long, flowing gowns from the next car boot sale and started calling everyone 'darling'; but this wasn't enough. What I really needed was a coffin. According to the book I found in the library, Sarah Bernhardt's coffin was almost as famous as she was. She would sleep in it whenever she was preparing for a tragic role or her tuberculosis-riddled sister was staying with her. In the postcard that I now had blu-tacked to my dressing table mirror, she was lying in it surrounded by flowers and love letters. I was certain that in order to prepare for my audition, I also needed to sleep in my own coffin.

Surprisingly, my parents were less convinced. They thought I should concentrate on learning a monologue. I tried persuading them that I would be unable to give an authentic performance in the audition without coming to terms with my own mortality, but they wouldn't budge. I dreamed of the day when I could leave home and move to London. When guests arrived for one of our numerous parties, my terribly bohemian flatmate would answer the door, cocktail in hand, wearing a kimono and announce,

'She's in her blasted coffin again!'

I did concede that my parents had a point about learning a speech. 'To be or not to be' seemed an obvious choice, as Hamlet was the only role I wanted to be considered for, and it would give me an opportunity to show off my emotional range. I liked the bit about your flesh feeling too solid, I could understand that. I practiced in the mirror whenever I could hear the television was on loud enough downstairs. By the time the audition came around, I was actually feeling pretty confident. The audition was afterschool, so I packed my costume in my backpack.

When the school bell finally rang and I was released from the torment of quadratic equations, I rushed to the toilets to change. I had swiped a pair of my mum's best tights from the washing machine. They were 80 denier and from Marks and Spencer so despite the fact that my mum was a couple of sizes smaller than me, I was fairly confident my knickers would not be visible. I had also taken one of my dad's two good shirts and the overall effect was as close as I could get to a doublet and hose. I tied my hair back in a bun and drew on some stubble with eye liner. I was possibly a little heavy-handed but I hoped that under the stage lights it wouldn't look as bad and would give my jaw a more masculine look. When I walked into the school hall it went very quiet. The drama teacher, Mr Harper, opened his mouth and then quickly closed it again. I could hear whispering. I presumed this was something I would have to get used to now I was becoming a star.

People were called onto the stage one at a time to recite their speeches whilst Mr Harper made notes. Most of them were awful. The boys mumbled and the girls fiddled with their hair. When they were finished Mr Harper would say a few words of encouragement but personally I couldn't see why he was being so nice to them all, he was only giving them false hope. Izzy Jenkins got the biggest round of applause. She was the prettiest and therefore most popular girl in my year. Her rendition of Juliet's 'Come gentle night' was so breathy that I thought Mr Harper was going to have to call a halt to the proceedings; you couldn't put that in front of the school governors. So, if anything, when my name was called I was grateful to have the opportunity to show them all how it should be done. I could hear whispering again as I made my way to the stage, but I ignored it; I was about to fulfil my destiny. I planted my feet firmly, projected my voice as best I could and used plenty of hand gestures. It was only when I took the first of my planned dramatic pauses that I heard the sniggering.

They were laughing at me. I could see Mr Harper turn around and stare at them warningly but still the sniggering continued. I could even hear some of the things they were saying. 'What the fuck is she doing?' 'What has she got on her face?' 'Have you seen the size of her thighs?' The stage lights were making me feel hot and sweaty. I couldn't remember my next line other than it had something to do with whips and scorn. I was pretty sure that Mr Harper had resorted to pretending to write things in his notebook. There was only one way out. I hurtled down the steps at the side of the stage, grabbed my backpack and ran. I ran straight out of the school and kept on running. I cut through the woods at the back of our housing estate, even though usually I was too scared to go there on my own in case I got molested by a stranger.

I wasn't used to running and had to slow down a bit because my lungs were hurting. I tried to wipe the snot off my face and promptly fell over a tree root. By the time I made it to my front door my dad's shirt was covered in mud, my mum's good tights were ruined and my hand was bleeding. Safe to say I was hysterical. After ascertaining that I hadn't in fact been molested by a stranger, my mum put me straight in the bath and made me a mug of Horlicks. Both she and my dad were remarkably good humoured about their ruined clothes but if anything, that made me feel worse. I knew that my humiliation was not something I could ever recover from. I also knew what was to blame. Everything would have been different if I'd had a coffin, and it had become more important than ever to get hold of one.

I came up with what I considered a simple yet brilliant plan. I decided to place an advertisement in the classified section of our local newspaper. It read: 'Wanted – one coffin, unused and preferably silk lined, must be able to deliver.' I planned to say, when I was inevitably questioned as to what I wanted with a coffin, that I was sourcing props for my school production of Hamlet. However, it's testament to the wide variety of items both proffered and sought by the area's residents, that when I rang to place my ad, the woman's voice didn't register the slightest surprise or even interest.

Unlike Izzy Jenkins, my parents couldn't afford to buy me a Nokia 3310 and saw no reason why I should need a mobile phone in the first place. So I had to put our landline on the ad and spend as much time as I could hovering near the phone to prevent my parents from answering. So closely did I guard the phone that my dad began to suspect, for the first time, that I might actually have a boyfriend. A whole, hellish week went past and the only person who called was a double glazing salesman. I resigned myself to spending lunchtimes locked in a toilet cubicle.

When the weekend finally came around, I dragged my duvet onto the sofa and had no intention of moving for the entire day. My mum had gone into town with my Aunty Sandra and my dad had gone to help his friend Steve with a DIY project, or as my mum predicted, drink pints in the shed. I was just deciding what to watch once Live and Kicking was finished when the phone went. I went for a sophisticated yet causal tone.

'Good morning, if it is still morning.'

'I hear you're in the market for a wooden overcoat.'

'I beg your pardon?'

'A coffin, love. My mate gave me this number, said you'd placed an ad for a coffin. Was he winding me up? I did wonder; he still hasn't forgiven me for the Christmas tree debacle.' Puzzled as I was by what this man could have possibly done with a Christmas tree, I was keen not to let the opportunity slip through my fingers.

'No, I do want a coffin, it's not a wind up.'

'Right, well, the old man's passed away and I've just discovered one in the loft.'

'Don't you want to use it for your dad?'

'We buried him last week, love. Only just started clearing out the house.'

'How much do you want for it?'

'Nothing.'

'You mean I can have it for free? Are you sure? Coffins are quite expensive, you know.'

'To be honest love, I'll be glad to see the back of it. As I said, I found it in the loft with some other things, personal things, photos and what have you, and I need to get rid of it before my mum finds out because I don't think she has any idea, bless her; it's certainly not her in any of the photos. Can't believe he was in to that stuff, kinky old sod. So basically you'd be doing me a favour by taking it off my hands. When shall I drop it round in the van?'

This was a lot to take in. It wasn't every day that a stranger revealed to you that their dad got up to what my mum insisted on calling hanky-panky, in a coffin, with a woman who wasn't his wife. I had also quite clearly

9

specified 'unused' in the advert. However, I decided
Sarah Bernhardt wouldn't be shocked; if anything, she'd
probably approve whole-heartedly. I would have to be more
openminded. I would also have to give it a good rub down
with the sterilising fluid my mum kept under the kitchen
sink when it arrived.

'Are you free now?'

I gave the man my address and he hung up. I didn't
even know his name, yet he would shortly be turning up
at the door and I was all by myself. I felt a bit scared. I
contemplated ringing Steve's house and asking my dad
to come home, but then I asked myself what would Sarah
Bernhardt do? So I ran upstairs, put on a floor-length velvet
dress and some of my mum's lipstick. A beaten up, old
transit van pulled up outside the house and I tried my best
not to think that it looked like the vehicle of a kidnapper.
I opened the door as the driver got out. He was short and
bald, which I found reassuring. Despite being shit at all
sports, I was what my dad would call a well-built girl, and I
was fairly confident that I could fend him off if push came
to shove.

'Alright love,' he yelled. 'Is your mum in?'

This threw me.

'No.'

'Oh, well I spoke to her about 15 minutes ago; she asked
me to drop something round.'

I thought fast, improvisation is a key skill for any actress.

'Yes, I know. She says she's really sorry, but she's had to
pop out, Nana's had a fall.'

Nana was actually sunning herself on the Costa del Sol
and no doubt already two vodka and cokes down, but I had
decided to play the sympathy card.

'She said you'd be dropping something round.'

'And did she tell you what it is?'

'Oh yes, Mum's done amateur dramatics for years. We're always having weird stuff turn up at the house. My dad helps with the sets.'

The man visibly relaxed and I delighted in my own deviousness. I hadn't anticipated quite how heavy coffins are, but he was puffing by the time he made it into the hallway. There was just about enough room for him to place it next to my bed, but he looked concerned again.

'Don't worry,' I assured him, 'we'll take excellent care of it.'

This did little to alter his expression, and he still look vaguely disturbed as he drove off. I closed the door and exhaled deeply; I could finally emulate my idol. I estimated I had a good hour to enjoy my new possession before Mum would be back from the shops, so I poured myself a glass of Ribena, which at least aesthetically resembled wine, and retired to my boudoir. The coffin wasn't exactly what I had envisaged. It looked like it was made from cheap pine instead of stained oak, and there were no fancy brass knobs or finials. A musty sort of smell emanated from the interior and I was disappointed to see there was no silk lining. Still, I thought, beggars can't be choosers. I fetched the sterilising fluid and a cloth, and gave the coffin, what my mum would call, a good going over.

At last, I delicately stepped inside and lowered myself down with as much grace as I could muster. It was a snug fit. Presumably the coffin had been made for someone already skeletal, because it took a fair amount wiggling to get my bum in. The idea that anyone could get up to hanky-panky in such a confined space made the mind boggle. I laid back and tried to imagine I was dead. I thought of my blood turning cold and my face growing pale. I thought of my heartbroken family tearfully laying flowers. I thought of Mr Harper vowing to never forgive himself for failing to recognise a bright yet fleeting talent. Sustaining such morbid fantasies is thirsty work, so I went to reach for my Ribena on the bedside table, which was when I discovered that I was stuck. I strained and I heaved. I could feel my pulse racing and I tried not to panic but it was no good; I was wedged firmly in the coffin like a cork in a bottle.

I had no choice but to lie there. I could hear kids playing outside but I was too embarrassed to yell for help and doubted whether they would hear me anyway. My imagination started to run away with itself. What if no one came home for hours? What if my dad had fallen asleep in a deck chair after one too many pints? What if Aunty Sandra was having man troubles again and my mum was forced to listen to her for ages over a frothy coffee? What if I needed a poo? Or worse, what if they didn't come home at all? What if my dad had had a freak DIY accident and was now lying in a hospital bed in a coma? What if my mum had secretly been having an affair with someone from work and run away to start a new life in Swindon? What if I actually died in this coffin and no one was here to even see it?

When I heard the key in the lock I cried with relief. And when my mum burst into the room, having hurtled up the stairs, spurred on by my hollering, she also cried, but with laughter. She laughed for a while. It took her quite a long time to actually get the words out when she rang my dad to tell him to hurry on home. The only small mercy was that there was no film left in the camera and my parents could not retain any hard evidence of my stupidity. When they eventually managed to lever me out, I did the tiniest of farts but luckily it was a silent one. It was a thoughtful suggestion of my dad's to use the coffin to build a bonfire.

As I watched the coffin burn and felt the glow from the fire warm my face, I vowed that from that day on I would be my own idol. I accepted a backstage role on the production of Hamlet and even managed to congratulate Izzy Jenkins on her competent, if simpering, performance as Ophelia. She even managed to say that I should wear all black more often. I got through my exams, and a long and glorious summer lay ahead of me. On the first weekend of the holidays my parents dragged me to, you guessed it, another car boot sale. And that was the day that changed my life; that was the day I miraculously found a copy of Bjork's latest, and greatest, album Vespertine for less than five pounds. I knew at once she was everything I wanted to be; artistic, avantgarde and undeniably sexy. And that is why I have a stuffed swan around my neck. And do you know what? Up yours if you don't like it.

Sometimes, A Girl

Ginna Wilkerson

Ginna Wilkerson has a Ph.D. in English from the University of Aberdeen. She has one poetry collection, Odd Remains, published in 2013. Currently, Ginna lives and works in Tampa, Florida. She can be contacted via email at ginnawilkerson@gmail.com.

I recall the theatre from once upon a moon.
I've entered this door, sat in the seat worn gray from blue,
watched this stage of somber midnight curtain.
A casket owns the center, a pre-emptory place for death,
or at least a show of dying like curtain time down.

Her service begins with sparse tones of dry sorrow
and subtle discomfort from the gathered few.
Tossed around the random hall, lights low for effect...
is it funeral or misbegotten musical, which or
what? gentle *port de bras* rises from the casket.

A hush falls like samaras from helicopter maples.
She appears from the depths and stands erect,
portly as proper for a matriarchal corpse - not
a corpse, but alive with inappropriate hair and
crown of carpet tacks like tiny swords.

Dancing feels like magic in this place of questions.
She dances, leaving the stage for seats unknown
where I had a girlfriend, or maybe sometimes, a girl
with the scent of lavender-incensed clothes.
Did she dance away? Did she die down and out?

Our copper-crowned dancer moves closer.
I can feel her shadow dancing like a memory lost.
She's all I have now that the girl has gone - all
there is here in my theatre of shaky starts.
A horn-ed moon hangs, like Shakespeare, over all.

I Am Beautiful

Ursula Woodcock

Ursula is a 22-year-old BA English student, currently in her final year of university. She enjoys creative writing, blogging, and talking about all things pop culture! In 2019 she began a 12-month marketing internship in East London, working for a boutique social media agency, where she gained valuable insight into the world of marketing and communications. In her spare time, she enjoys watching documentaries, going to the theatre, and exploring the quirkiest bars and restaurants London has to offer.

'Finn! Catch yourself on! If you think you're going to start your sixth form years late you've got another thing coming. Out of bed and downstairs for breakfast in five.'

I wasn't sure what was worse - my mammy's constant screeching at 7.00 am or the thought of stepping back into that hole for another year.

St Aidan's was the largest school in Ballycastle. It was also the typical secondary school cliché, filled with rough lads who only cared about football and the school's female population. I was obsessed with girls too though. I was obsessed with their hair, I was obsessed with their clothes, the way they spoke, their bodies, their minds.

I slithered down the stairs, half-dressed, and taking in the smell of crispy bacon and burned toast.

My mammy was juggling between watching the stove, ironing my uniform and plaiting my sister's hair.

'Take your trousers, Finn.'

My heart sank. She must have seen the disappointment in my eyes.

'Don't start, love. It was okay during the summer, when nobody could see you, but its term time now and these are the rules.'

I snatched the trousers out of her hands, immediately feeling guilty. It wasn't her fault; it wasn't anybody's fault. It was just the way I was. The next half an hour was spent detaching every inch of my personality and leaving it in my bedroom until four o'clock that afternoon. Stripping the bright orange nail polish from my hands was the final wave goodbye to summer.

I was eight-years-old when I realized. My twin sisters Aiofe and Roisin were playing dress up. It was their chosen activity most days; our humble lounge became something resembling a drag queen's dressing room, and each fraction of our carpet was covered with feather bowers, sparkly dresses and endless piles of costumes. Even my ma's 25-year-old wedding dress had begrudgingly been donated once she had realized that the twins were sneaking into her wardrobe at any given opportunity to try it on. Whilst our walls had more glitter and makeup on them than my sister's actual faces, and the outfits were more boot sale bargains than catwalk couture, nothing could compare to the look in their eyes, filled with joy as they became someone else for the afternoon. From mermaids to princesses, lions to fairies, sometimes even their favourite pantomime villains reared their ugly heads. Demand a character, animal or even an inanimate object and within minutes they were able to dive into their box and become someone else. Unfortunately, there was no alter-ego on earth for eight-year-old boys to hide behind, even if it was just for the afternoon.

The heavens opened on my way to school, and whilst this was typical of a September morning in Northern Ireland, I couldn't help but think it was pathetic fallacy. Approaching the bus stop was always a troublesome activity; the so-called 'cool lads' would take up every inch of the pavement, smoking, shoving each other, and hurling general abuse at any poor sod who happened to walk by.

'Ya wee gay freak,' was the first of many insults chucked at me that morning. It actually made me smirk a little. I wasn't gay. If anything, I hated the male species.

I sighed, stepped onto the bus and headed to my usual spot by the driver. It was safest there. It was only when I had practically dumped my backside on the seat that I realized that it was already occupied by a complete stranger.

'Oh ... I'm sorry!' I exclaimed, embarrassed at the thought of the poor wee girl enduring my arse in her face first thing in the morning.

'No bother,' she replied, fixing the hair clip that I had somehow managed to mess up.

The embarrassment soon turned to envy. How would I style my hair if I had the freedom to grow it long? My own thick, dark hair was kept short, in line with the school dress code, despite my desires to grow luscious locks like that Harry Styles fella. She must have noticed my daydreaming.

'Did you want to sit next to me?' the stranger asked, moving her bag from the seat.

'That would be grand. Thanks.'

A few awkward minutes passed before I managed to pluck up the courage to ask who this mysterious girl was, and what she was doing on the 8.15 am bus to St Aidan's.

Her name was Ciara, and she had moved here from Kilkenny at the end of the Summer. She had wild curly hair and electric green eyes. I could see that each of her nails were painted a different colour of the rainbow, clashing beautifully with the marron blazer sleeve they were hiding under.

I didn't want to mention that wearing nail polish resulted in a one-hour detention with Sister Nadine … I would know, I'd endured many myself.

We talked for the next half an hour about anything and everything. Our favourite shows, what music we liked and how we couldn't wait to leave school, travel and never talk about Pythagoras Theorem again. I hadn't felt this comfortable with someone for a long time and it felt nice, almost freeing. Most of my school days were spent on my own, surrounded by people who thought farting in the middle of class was the height of comedy. I didn't have any friends, and I certainly didn't have anyone who understood me.

'You're different to other boys, aren't you Finn?' she said as the bus pulled up outside the school gates. A soft smile grew across her face. I think it was a compliment.

I smiled back at her.

'You have no idea.'

Ciara soon became my best friend. She was unique like me, although granted maybe not on the same level. She didn't care about what other girls thought of her. She didn't care that she wasn't definition of 'pretty' or that boys would make fun of her bright purple glasses and love of fantasy books. That's what I loved so much about her. I felt as though I could tell her anything, even the one thing that only my closest family knew. I wasn't happy in my body.

It was an evening in November that I decided to tell her my biggest secret. She had invited me over to stay the night for the first time and I knew I couldn't hide it any longer. For the last five years of school I had kept it hidden from the whole of the student population, with my days spent dreaming of how I would look if I were to transition, or the euphoria I would finally feel when I dressed exactly how I liked and acted the way I knew I was born to act. Wearing nail polish and stealing my sister's makeup were all temporary pleasures, but telling someone outside the four walls of my family home, that was permanent.

I'd been to Ciara's house a few times for tea and movie nights, but never to stay over.

'I'm not having my wean invite a fella into her bedroom under my roof,' Ciara's da would reply at the notion of me staying the night. Ciara and I were just friends of course, but this was Northern Ireland and despite whatever my head and heart were telling me, to them I was a fella. I had been reassured that her parents were away for the weekend, and I was more than welcome to keep her company, so I did.

'Hey bestie!'

Her friendly nature immediately put me at ease, and I

felt as though I was making the right decision telling her.

'Head upstairs, I'll grab us some wee drinks.'

I made my way to her bedroom which was undoubtably my favourite room of her house, mainly because of her whacky wardrobe and extensive makeup collection. My inability to express who I really was led my own clothes to consist of the same basic t-shirts and jeans, and any makeup I ever experimented with was my sister's sloppy seconds. I couldn't help myself from opening the wardrobe and taking a look at each of the items folded neatly inside; the desperation to try something on was almost unbearable. Luckily, I noticed the sound of Ciara's footsteps edging closer, so I slammed the door and practically dived onto her bed to avoid any unwanted suspicion.

'Here you go, it's a Ciara special!' she exclaimed, passing me the suspicious concoction.

I took one sip and almost gagged; clearly the freedom of Ciara's parents being away had led her to delve deep into their alcohol cabinet.

'What the feck is in that?' I laughed as I placed the cup on the side, refusing to touch it again, although the high alcohol content would certainly provide some of the Dutch courage I was desperately after. Maybe I was wrong to tell her; what if she thought of me differently? What if she thought I was a freak?

'Ciara, I need to tell you something.'

She inched towards me, suddenly looking concerned.

'What's up?'

'I've wanted to tell you this for a while, but I never knew how to. Please know that I'm still me on the inside, nothing has changed in that way. I've known I was different for years, but its only now that I've felt comfortable to tell someone other than my family. Look ...the thing is ...'

'It's okay Finn, you can tell me anything no matter what.

Take a deep breath and say it ... unless it's that you're secretly a Hufflepuff, best to keep that to yourself.'

Her jokes made me even more nervous. No, I wasn't a Hufflepuff (which was an insult to all Harry Potter fans alike) but I was keeping a secret.

Clinging onto her bed sheets for some kind of comfort, I opened my mouth and began to speak.

'I feel like I'm trapped in my body. I can't bear the way I look or who I am, and I know I was never meant to live like this. I want to transition. I want to be me.'

It was then that the tears started to stream from my eyes, as if they would never stop. No matter how hard I tried, I couldn't get any other words out and looking up seemed like the most difficult action in the world. After what felt like a lifetime, I slowly raised my eyes, to see Ciara in tears herself. Edging towards me, she took my hands and lightly kissed my cheek.

'I love you Finn. No matter what.'

That night was spent talking about how I felt, and what the next steps were going to be. Ciara was amazing, listening to each word so deeply and comforting me when I would break down in tears. How had I been lucky enough to have a best friend like her? She was understanding, gentle and spoke to me with such respect that any remaining shame or embarrassment I consumed left my body almost instantly. I had this amazing companion, who I could totally be myself around and although I wasn't ready to come out to the rest of the world, I felt safe knowing that she loved me for me.

The next week of school was filled with the usual drivel, including an hour-long assembly with Sister Nadine. She was a large woman, with a frightfully strong Belfast accent and a face that never seemed to change its irritated expression.

'Sure, the annual Christmas Dance is next Friday, where we will be raising money for the new chairs in the chapel. Tickets are available from the reception desk; no drinking, no funny business and if you're late you're not getting in. Now, let us pray.'

The dance soon became the hot topic of conversation across the school, and whilst everyone else was excited at the thought of getting dressed up and awkwardly dancing around our gymnasium, I was filled with dread. That didn't matter though, because I wasn't going, I never did.

'You're not going?' Ciara exclaimed on the bus home.

'Ay, I hate all that craic, it's just the same asses we see every day at school, but in suits and dresses.'

'Don't be such a killjoy! It'll be fun and we can go together if you'd like … and get ready together?'

I knew what she was hinting at, and I wasn't having any of it.

'Catch yourself on! Ciara, if you think I'm going to walk into the school dance dressed like a contestant from Ru Paul's drag race then you have another thing coming.'

'I'm not going to push it, but I know you wouldn't let your best friend in the whole world go on her own, now, would you?'

She winked, grabbed her bag and jumped off the bus.

Despite the idea of going to the Christmas Dance making me feel slightly ill, I wanted to do something nice for Ciara to thank her for being there for me recently. She didn't have dances at her old school, so I understood why she wanted to attend. There was one problem: if I was going to the dance, I was going as the real me.

'It's arrived!' my mammy shouted from the bottom of the stairs.

It was the evening of the dance, and the nerves were

eating me alive.

'You're so brave, my love, and you're going to look absolutely grand. I know I've told you that sometimes it's best to hide in order to protect yourself, but I was wrong. You are who you are, and you should never be ashamed of that,' she said softly, passing me the package whilst wiping a tear from her eye.

'Ay mammy, thank you. I love you.'

I rushed up to my room, shut the door, and opened the parcel to find a magnificent red dress, made to fit me perfectly. I slipped it on, and instantly burst into tears. This is what I had waited for. I wanted to feel beautiful, I wanted to feel feminine, and this dress made me feel nothing less. Luckily for me, I had two sisters on hand to help with my makeup.

'Now what are we going for today? Full on glam or a subtle glow?' Aiofe laughed, reaching for her brushes.

'You only come out to the whole of your school once, don't you? Let's make it worth it,' I replied, using humour to hide my horrific fears.

An hour passed and I was finally ready to leave, although I had repeatedly contemplated ripping off the dress, crawling back into bed and forgetting the whole idea entirely. It took one glance in the mirror for me to understand that I was doing the right thing.

I knocked on the door of Ciara's house, sweating so much that I feared my makeup was going to melt straight off my face. She answered, wearing a bright yellow dress and red converse. Typical Ciara.

'Finn, you look so beautiful.'

'It's Freya now,' I whispered.

Fit For A Queen

Rosie Cowan

Derry-born Rosie Cowan is a former Guardian Ireland crime correspondent, currently studying a PhD in Criminal Law at Queen's University Belfast. Her short story, Little Wren, was one of 10 prizewinners from 1,468 entries in the Fish international short story competition 2020 and is published in the Fish 2020 anthology. She recently completed a psychological thriller featuring a female crime reporter on a London-based national newspaper.

Make you stare, don't I? Make you wonder
Blow your tiny mind asunder
Scarlet starlet, I am fierce
Battle dress, I pierce
Your tunnel vision
Burst your bubble, that's my mission
Classy, sassy, ghetto chic
She made me, she on fleek
In my sequins, she bares her soul
I fuse her broken pieces whole
That skinny kid you called fag and poof
I got her ass covered, she bulletproof

Versace, Harlem, Serengeti
I celebrate her DNA confetti
Send her gender flip to town
Bespoke gown for a new pronoun
Wearing me shows all her nerve
I cling to every curve
God didn't give her, hell no, she create her own
Now this princess fully grown

You think I conjure an illusion
No! Be under no delusion
Her inner beauty shines through me
I the shore, she the sea
I the dazzling shell, but she the pearl
I know the grit that formed the girl
Yeah, she been through some things
She coming out, she the butterfly, I her wings
Sista, we in this together, we slayin' this scene
I am fabulous, fit for my Queen.

D'Or, Golden Dor

Manuela Vitelaru

Manuela is 24 and currently a MA Creative Writing and Publishing student at Bournemouth University. She writes poems and short fiction inspired by the world around her, history and the arts. Her current fictional work in progress, 'Amid the Broken Reeds', is a reflective, compassionate account of a Roma artist who rediscovers herself after a traumatic experience of being human trafficked.

It's *soare cu dinti*: a crisp, sunny morning of early spring,
the ninth of March more precisely, *Mucenici* or Christian
Martyrs Day. I should be feeling *hopeful* now that I've
made it through my third harsh winter in Romania.
Yet I have mixed feelings of *dor*, excitement, and fear.
I'm nervous about Mr. Dumitrescu's class of Applied
Linguistics and Literature starting in half an hour.
Rumours among students at Transilvania University say
that Mr. Dumitrescu stopped ageing in December '89 once
communism fell. To me, it's his mentality that seems not
to have changed since. That's why he hates Blaga and will
also hate my Blagian inspired poems for today. 'You won't
graduate this year, Hope!' He often tells me with an evil
grin. As I'm waiting in front of the seminar room, I wonder
whether I could ever win Mr. Dumitrescu's favour just
once. Yet, how could I? Unless I suggest a new hypothesis
for the etymological and semantic mystery of Romanian
dor as coming from the French *d'or*, but who would take
me seriously? What do students know? Surely, they're
not as great, not as brave, and certainly not as free as the
deep thinkers and poets who expanded and explored the
complex meaning of *dor* throughout the centuries. I *hope*
that my poems stir up *dor* — a *dor* which feels like the
emptiness within us in times of loneliness and grief, but
stronger and deeper; a *dor* that resembles the nostalgia
that you get from stories about memories. To me, *dor* (d'or)
is precious like my mum's golden jewellery box. It became
mine after she died of cancer. I remember how for years I
left it unopened, covered in dust by my bedroom window in
Worcester. Perhaps time slows down when you're waiting
and rushes on too fast in the face of death. I often wonder
how Dad was so patient with me growing up.

When I lived in England, I barely heard any Romanian
spoken outside my parents' house. I remember we used to

live on the corner of a small, cobbled street right behind Worcester Cathedral, where on late autumn afternoons the sun would softly warm brassy and golden leaves. At night, if I was at home, I could always hear rushing steps from my room, crushing and scattering these dried leaves, up and down from the town centre towards London Road. Many nights though, I was going out with college friends, and would come back very drunk after midnight, always to find Dad still awake. 'I'm living life to the fullest,' I'd think to myself. I couldn't care less about anything, even that Dad was a widower, carrying the burden of a medium-sized church on his shoulders. Dad used to paint on Saturday afternoons, but a stroke stole his creativity. Having an excellent memory now, Dad began writing church memoirs from the communist period instead. I grew weary of listening to him. I felt as though I was born in a prison — all that I'd heard and known my whole life was his and Mum's stories of faith. Although I wanted to escape, for some reason, it felt strange — it was too late. These stories had become mine, too. My reality. That in '86, like Mum and Dad, I too had fled communist Romania to preserve my faith — but really, what faith? A couple of days before Dad died, I was fortunate to have had one last chance to speak to him over the phone. It was the first time in three years.

'Dad,' I said, utterly failing to hide that I was upset, 'It's Hope ...'

'Mica mea draga, you know that I'm always here for you ...'

'Sorry I haven't phoned you in so long. I just want to tell you ... Please ... forgive me for hurting you and Mum. I miss you ...' I was supposed to travel back in my winter holiday to see him again, but it was too late— he had died one month later in November.

That weekend of October, the roads were closed due

to protests or strikes. I was stuck in Gara de Nord train station in Bucharest, which is one of the busiest and most dangerous parts of the capital, except for Ferentari and the suburbs. I was spending the day there to visit an art exhibition, but also to see with my own eyes the places that I'd heard about from my parents, like the Revolution Square and the Parliament Palace. Bucharest felt strangely familiar. I was also annoyed to see grey, tall socialist blocks of flats among beautiful, renaissance inspired buildings — why?! I was left without a choice but to spend the next two hours on a train next to an elderly man, Constantin, who was about 60 years old, and who proudly told me that he fought in the Decembrist Romanian revolution. His dark, pessimistic humour about today's politics and his small moustache reminding me of Hitler's made him intriguing, even suspicious.

'I used to teach Literature, you know. I even published several poems, some in my name, others in my friend's name ... Now tell me, where was your God in communism? What's the name of your sect again?' He told me. Each of his words sounded like he was reading someone else's speech, like I used to recite memorised bible verses at youth camps. His clothes stank of old *naftalina*. I was convinced that Constantin had never fought against the communists. Something about his mannerism was not right — he used his hands excessively. He insisted on convincing me about the bright side of communism, that only the leaders were evil, that people had jobs and the country wasn't in debt, that the crime rate was so much lower ...

'My God was beside all those suffering in prison, like my parents,' I said with much boldness as if this was a sort of truth he'd never heard of before and continued: 'Mr. Constantin, did you own a list? What were your poems about?' But he ignored all my questions and started swearing.

'Ah, *la naiba*! These trains are late! There're people here with high blood pressure!'

Perhaps, he might be an ex-communist spy that once reported his family, friends and neighbours for social status and his own safety. He must have compromised to the regime, not only his poetry but his own conscience, too. He may have very well been my parents' jail officer. This thought troubled me, so I went to the door of the old CFR train to see what was happening outside, as I could hear people arguing. Typically, some were fighting just in front of the pretzel shop which I had left five minutes before, and people gathered around to watch them. The police certainly wouldn't come; I had learnt that by then. They looked like they belonged to a mafia group who facilitate human trafficking to England and of which you rarely hear.

It is unusual for foreigners, they say, to come and study at Transilvania University and many wondered why I was able to speak Romanian so well, even though I had a slightly strange accent. Recently, I was surprised when Cristi, probably the brightest guy in my class, came up to me in one of the breaks, and said:

'Hope,' sounding rather intrigued, 'Why did you move here? It's thirty years now since the country's democratic ... everyone wants to leave, especially young people like us, and you come here!'

He normally spends his free time preparing for university debates on democracy and freedom of speech or does private Greek tutoring for theology students, despite being an atheist himself; he rarely hangs out with any of us. He's thin and tall with very short, blond hair, cut 'periuta' style like a Russian soldier, and wears baggy, old clothes that everyone says were his older brother's. This is Cristi.

'Nu-ti mai place romana, Cristi?' I replied, suggesting

jokingly that he can speak Romanian to me. 'I love it here, you know, but I think that communism has sadly been followed by an even deeper corruption than the country has ever seen. It's almost like going to the doctor to have a cancerous tumour removed and then another one springs up in a different part of your body. It's that seed of corruption that we all need a cure for.'

'I can see clearly now that there's something different about you, Hope, that something's changed. You're carrying a sense of hope, a special aura ... what's this all about?' Then Cristi took out a closed envelope from his backpack and explained, 'You see this? That's how I'm securing my first place for teaching after masters. There's no other way. There's no hope in this country!

'People here started realising that the corruption left by communism is endemic and has no cure, that it leaves such deep wounds on the culture and in people's mentality. Never mind, I have to go,' Cristi said abruptly, rushing towards the teachers' room.

In fact, I never felt Romanian, nor did I ever feel British. Growing up between two languages and two cultures, my heart had been torn between the two. It's never been easy. So many times, I felt clumsy in my use of either English or Romanian — mixing up words, mispronouncing them with strange accents, swapping syntax and using the wrong kind of mannerisms in conversations with native speakers. My family's exile became my home and what used to be their home I made to be my kind of 'exile', to the point that now I don't know where I belong. 'That's OK, I guess. We're not meant to belong here. Our home is heaven, we're just like a passing mist through this world ...' I thought to myself, but it clearly sounded like something Dad would tell me. I would often make up in my mind, from memories, his loving voice telling me something like: 'Hope, you're free to do what you want, but be wise in your freedom and trust me.' Today I understand that all Dad wanted for me was the best. Today he'd be so proud of me, of my poetry and of my relationship with our Hungarian relatives in Transylvania, who can't speak Romanian although they've lived in Romania for longer than I have— *Szeretlek! Megoszthatjuk Erdélyt*!

I wish I had been born in communism, if that had meant seeing the joy on my parents' faces as they watched the sun setting over communist Bucharest one evening of January '86, as their Swiss plane was taking off to Berne. Their faith had been tested and they were even ready to die in prison. Yet my teenage lifestyle had been one of disobedience and disrespect towards them. I wish I'd heard the hope in their voices! That first breakfast watching the sunrise in freedom again! Then I was born. They called me Hope because I was born in a free country.

I realise that Mr. Dumitrescu's class should start in less than five minutes. I quickly get my creative writing notebook out of my small flowery bag, in which all I can fit is my lunch box and some History books. I go through the two modernist poems for today's seminar and ensure that the Romanian and English read well.

(Romanian poem, translated:)
I only wish you were mine and I was yours.
Belonging to you wholly.
On whispers of springs, softly
Calling you. On wailing melodies of exile, torture
Oh, to forsake you — Forgotten
In memories from communist times.
Oh, cruel exile! How hard it is for one like me
To be born a foreigner in my own 'Home'.
I can't bow down to and worship the graves

Of Lenin and of Stalin — wait, what's this?
To me it stinks of pine! Nonsense!
This is rose perfume: Wild, red, so fragile —
But crushed, dried! Ouch!
Crushed with thorns as well ...
Too late, too late. They're dead already also.
Those thorns remind me of *The World's Corolla of Wonders*
That which was once hidden, forbidden
Yet not forgotten, of Blaga's.
Finally, dear *comrade*, if find boldness, courage —
I forgive you, truly! Now one last thing I'm left with,
It's hard to forget and believe —
You made me a foreigner in my own land.
Oh, cruel exile, receive me home!

(English Poem:)
Oh love, I wish I knew you from before
As being mine, forevermore; a refuge, exile
So hoped for — a promised land I dreamt about
One day I will belong to
Wholly, just as I am. Rapidly
Running towards you
Like streams of water. 'Here I am! All yours
In full surrender!' Softly calling you ...
One day I really hope
No longer will I thirst when certainly I know
Your water's good for me to drink, I heard —
Your water's free — All paid for!
Let me just build my corner to your table.
I might be late if that's okay?
But surely coming to your feast! Let me just ...
You know, help you, just in case!
Perhaps I could add something worth of praise
Something of value that you lack, to add

To what you've done! What lies!
Or better shall I drink This golden cup waiting for me
Of glory and of pain, despair, much shame,
Amongst some precious stones
Like rubies, diamonds and sapphires.

What would Mr. Dumitrescu say about my poems? I can
either finish brilliantly or fail, or perhaps use an envelope
like Cristi, but how could I compromise my freedom and
integrity to such an extent? That's it then. I will fail. *Dor*,
golden *d'or*, what have you done to me?

Dor feels like something which words apart from *dor*
can't describe. I'm reminded from Mr. Dumitrecu's class
about the *dor* explored in Romanian folklore: in pastoral
and heroic poems sung in hymns, *doine* and ballads, all
calling for a place of rest and a deeper sense of freedom and
belonging, an idealised love; a longing for something more
than what we have and know! As if it were eternity that the
heart of every person sought ...

Perhaps *dor* simply calls for *hope*. I'm feeling *hopeful*
as I hear the nightingale chirping, here commonly known
as *the spring's herald*. Even though I can't see it, it must
be somewhere close to the window because I can hear it.
Nature also finds hope after a long winter — although just
temporarily — and even migratory birds can eventually
return to where they belong. Our campus has a lovely view
to the old town centre, where history is told through bullet
scarred buildings from the Revolution and cobbled streets
on which Blaga probably rushed to hide from security. Even
the Festival Pub was once an underground writing and
philosophy club that secretly published uncensored literary
magazines, and even pocket-sized Bibles with random book
covers, for Russian soldiers who came to faith in Christ.
I see Cristi, Vlad and Maria rushing into the university

building. *Hopefully*, they will enjoy my poems.

Winchester In My Pocket

Early 1990s in democratic Romania

Manuela Vitelaru

Manuela is 24 and currently a MA Creative Writing and Publishing student at Bournemouth University. She writes poems and short fiction inspired by the world around her, history and the arts. Her current fictional work in progress, 'Amid the Broken Reeds', is a reflective, compassionate account of a Roma artist who rediscovers herself after a traumatic experience of being human trafficked.

Among poets, there's smoke—
a goddess with cigarettes of import
strong and fearless,
she covers my bruised mind
with a soft, white mist...
Her breath, a summer breeze,
blows my verses like ashes
down on white valleys
of Winchester lilies.

Among poets, there're pockets—
I buried my pen and creased my paper
cold and shaking,
my withered palm closes
I'm even more scared now...
Would they forget me?
Would anybody find my voice
in silver buttoned denim shirts
of washed-out blue ink?

A Bowl Of Pho

Belinda Weir

Belinda Weir is a writer and poet, originally from Scotland, now living in the North of England. She has published stories in the 'Northern Crime One' anthology, the Scholastic 'Short Stories for Children' anthology, and poems in Dust poetry magazine. She's also been longlisted for the 1000-word challenge competition in 2019, highly commended in the Poetry on the Lake competition in 2018 and shortlisted for the 'To Hull & Back' competition in 2019. Belinda blogs about systems, complexity, hedgehogs and foxes, and leadership, and has worked for the NHS for most of her career.

I had no idea when I met Linh that she would spend the rest of her life with me.She was very beautiful. 'Out of your league, Bao,' I thought to myself. I had no hope of attracting her, so I was able to be myself with Linh. I made her laugh. Silly jokes – taking a coin out of my bag and making it disappear, only to "find" it again nestling in her trouser pocket. Making fart noises so everyone thought the guy next to me had broken wind, that sort of thing. It was worth the possibility of getting into trouble, just to hear Linh giggle. They say that women like men who are funny, provided they are not fat as a porker and ugly as Uncle Wen I suppose. What do I know? I have not known many women, but even I could tell that Linh was special.

I saw her properly just twice, once when we boarded and again when we stopped, and it was dark both times, with only brief shafts of sudden moonlight, but her face is burned in my memory. Her hair hung straight and fine in a bob that stopped just short of her jawline, and her fringe was long so that she seemed to peep from under it, with big eyes, black and shiny as molasses. Her skin was smooth and pale as buttermilk. I thought when I first saw her that she was a little chubby. It was surprising – her bulky arms and tummy seemed at odds with the bird-like wrists and slender fingers that emerged from the cuffs of her pink jumper.

'I put on all my clothes,' she confided. 'I didn't want to leave any behind, and I thought it might be cold in London.'

That explained why she felt so soft when I put my arm around her. She was padded like a marshmallow – a vest, a long-sleeved blue t-shirt, then a green silk blouse with a peter pan collar, a white collarless shirt over that, then the pink jumper and finally a huge waterproof jacket like a quilt, black so that it didn't reflect light, and with a hood to cover her face. In the darkness I could feel her breath on my cheek when she turned to whisper to me, and when she lay her head down on my shoulder to sleep, I could sense her heart beating, just a few centimetres away from mine.

'Where are you from?' she asked me. She spoke in a low voice but even so, someone at the other side admonished her. 'Quiet!'

The unit was sealed; nothing could get in or out and unless we stood up and started banging on the walls, nobody would know we were in there. We had been told to make no sound, no noise at all. I knew that if anyone heard us, they might send us home and all the waiting and the planning, the hard work and the saving, the goodbyes and good luck conversations, all of it would have been for nothing. But it made no difference because Linh couldn't stop talking. Every few seconds a thought would occur to her, which she had to share.

'Do you think we'll see the Queen when we get to London?' she asked me.

Then, a little later, 'I will get a job in a bar when we get there. There are lots of bars, and they pay well, Tranh said.'

Tranh was her brother. Linh had told me, in an earlier burst of confidence, that he did not have a proper job, but worked at the beach bar, collecting glasses, washing up, stacking away the wooden tables and chairs. It was his idea, Linh told me, that she should make the journey first. They had saved tips for a long time, Linh said. She had told me many things about herself during the long journey, while I had shared nothing.

My brother impressed that on me when I called to say goodbye. He silently ladled me a bowl straight from the huge restaurant wok.

I wanted to enjoy the pho, savour the juicy chicken, the crunch of the sprouts, the sharp eye-watering bite of the spring onion.

But there was no time. I shovelled the chewy noodles into my mouth, trying not to slurp the salty broth, and even so I splashed a little on my t-shirt.

'Keep your head down Bao, okay? Just keep your mouth shut and you'll be fine,' Huy instructed.

Head down, mouth shut. Right. After a pause, when I was turning my attention once more to chasing the last bite of chicken round the bowl, he said,

'You're on your own, Bao. Don't forget that. Don't trust anyone.' He punched me on my shoulder, and said, 'Take it easy, man,' and went back to his cooking.

I smiled in the darkness – I could almost taste that pho.

Linh turned around, shifting her weight to lean in closer to me, so we were curled up like spoons. It was not because she liked me, she said, but because she was cold. We all were, at first, freezing, and Linh, beneath all her tops and shirts, was thin too. Tiny.

'If you won't tell me anything about you, tell me a story. I'm scared,' she said.

'No Linh. We really shouldn't be talking,' I scolded her.

Linh sniffed and said, into the darkness,'I thought we were going to be friends. I will tell you about my life then, Mr Boring. And no, you will not shhh me. I like to talk – it stops my teeth from chattering. I come from a little fishing village in the north. It is – it used to be – very beautiful, a lovely place. We have long beaches of fine soft sand, like palm sugar, the greenest sea and the nicest people. Everyone knows everyone. Everyone talks to anyone, there are no strangers in my village. Even in the summer, when there are tourists, it's a good place to live. My father is a fisherman – or he was for a long time, and my brother, Tranh, was too. Every morning they would sail out, very early, when the sky was still dark and only the tiniest hint of morning on the horizon, in daddy's little wooden boat, to catch fish. I would go down to the shore to watch them casting off sometimes.'

The guy on my other side was listening too. I could hear his breathing slowing down – he had been very scared when we first climbed in, almost crying, and I think he would have run off if the driver hadn't picked him up by the collar and pretty much thrown him into the van like a sack of beets.

'Too late for second thoughts,' the driver had said. Now the boy lay curled up on his side, and he shuffled across the floor till his back was against my leg for warmth. I pushed him away a little – I only wanted to feel Linh close to me. It was not polite of me, I know that, and I wish I had been kinder.

'There isn't much to do in the village, but that's okay,' said Linh. 'Mum died when I was quite little, so I look after the house, I do the cooking and take Minh to school, I clean a bit, work in a bar sometimes in the evening, watch TV – the usual kind of thing.'

'Is that why you left? It was dull?'

I was interested, despite myself.

I felt Linh stiffen next to me. 'It wasn't dull,' she corrected me. 'Peaceful. Nice. I liked it.'

She was quiet for a few minutes.

'So...'

'So, there was an accident a few months ago – a chemical spill from one of the factories somewhere further up the coast. We didn't find out for a while, but the fish started dying. They floated in on every tide, thousands of them, bellies up and gasping. Papa said we couldn't eat them. He couldn't catch healthy fish so that was that. No more work for Daddy or for Tranh. And no tourists because the beaches were spoiled. So, no money.'

Linh said nothing again for a long while. She pulled

her knees up to her chin and rested her head on them. I thought maybe she was crying but if she was, she at least did it silently.

After a few minutes she turned her head, and I could feel her looking at me.

'Still, new life, eh?' I could tell she was smiling.

'Yes,' I said.

For what felt like hours then, there was silence. We lay still, waiting. Listening. I allowed myself to feel the warmth of Linh next to me, imagined that it could go on, that we would be friends after our journey ended. She will need a friend, I thought, and why not Bao? She had grown to trust me in the tiny space of time we had been together, and I thought we could spent the rest of our lives together. If not as a boyfriend, I could be like a brother to her. I did not want to be on my own, that's the truth.

I must have slept eventually because I dreamed about my mother. She was cooking in the tiny kitchen, using the only ring that worked; the burners were clogged, and the flames sputtered and danced under the wok. She turned to me, smiled, and pulled me to her for a hug.

'My Bao,' she whispered. She hugged me closer, and then tighter, crushing me, making it difficult to breathe. When I fought my way out of sleep and opened my eyes to the blackness, I realized that part of the dream was true – I was finding it hard to catch a breath. I stood up, my head swimming, tried to bang on the side of the van.

There was a rasping noise behind me, one of the others whispering,

'I can't breathe. Help.'

I wanted to help. But I had no strength for anything; as weak as a drowning kitten, I had just enough time to lower myself to the floor, wrap my arms around Linh and hope that dying wouldn't hurt too much, before everything went black.

I really don't remember anything after that. Not until I woke up in the hospital. It seems I was one of the fortunate ones, although I don't feel lucky. They are planning to send me back, as soon as I am well enough to travel. Sooner, probably.

I overheard the nurses talking next to my bed last night.

'Imagine, dying like that. Far away from home, in the dark, among strangers. Whatever would make you do such a thing?'

I wanted to say something, but I didn't want them to know I could understand what they were saying.

'The girl he was with,' said the nurse, not looking at me as she attached a bag of fluid to the pole at the head of the bed. 'Do you think she was his girlfriend?'

And that is how I learned that Linh was dead.

The women looked at each other; the younger one shook her head. They both finished what they were doing without speaking and went away to attend to other patients.

Later in the evening the older nurse came back, holding a plastic bag. She pulled the curtains shut around my bed and handed it to me silently; I expected food, maybe a book or some soap perhaps.

It wasn't soap. Or food. Inside the bag were Linh's clothes: a vest, a long-sleeved blue t-shirt, a green silk blouse with a peter pan collar, a white collarless shirt, a pink jumper and, on the top, a waterproof jacket, size large, black and padded.

The nurse left, and I got up. I took the drip from my arm and I found my jeans and t-shirt in the grey metal locker next to the bed. I put those on, catching the faintest scent of sour, salty noodle broth as I pulled the t-shirt over my head. Over the top I slipped on Linh's jacket. I gathered the hood around my face and waited until I could hear that the nurses were busy with the old man who was dying, quietly, in the room next door. I picked up the bag, walked down the rubber floor of the corridor in bare feet, pressed the button to release the door, and stepped out into the night.

One day I will go to Linh's village, and I will tell her father, and Tranh, that Linh told me all about them and how much she loved them, and that when Linh died, she was excited and happy and looking forward to a new life. And she was among friends. Till then, I will wear her jacket. I don't think she would mind.

Pilgrim

Julia Chmielowska

Julia Chmielowska wrote throughout her childhood in New York, summers in Poland and travels around Europe following her family's move to London. After a brief break from creativity to study physics at university, she rediscovered her love of sharing stories with others, and has been writing around her job ever since. She can be contacted at julia.chmielowska@gmail.com.

The night settles in, clouds low. Beneath the pines
I make my home. Sunset light reflects just so - I feel the urge
To dive beneath the frozen lake.
I breathe, inhale the icy air,
Exhale a mist that rises, fades, disappears. A fog rolls in
Down from the hills; something about it feels like an embrace.
I contemplate
The thousand miles that lie
In my wake. Countries, continents, cities, roads;
From each I have taken, enriched my soul.
Each one, it has left me a little less whole, yet still
I know, as sure as my feet will tread through new snow
As the next years come and the next years
Go, as sure as the bonfire spreads its warmth through my bones,
I'll carry on following the flow of my blood,
The dance and the song that with it comes.
I'll follow this rhythm through the magic bright lights
Just as I've followed it here, to the depths of the night.

A Day In Madrid

Helen Lawrence

*Helen is a solicitor by profession, and lives and works in
Edinburgh. She is one of the many people all over the world
who took up writing during the pandemic. She picked up a
(metaphorical) pen when furloughed in March, discovered not
just a hobby but a passion, and has been making up for lost time
ever since. She can be contacted at hl20122016@gmail.com.*

'It's a bit like that film, isn't it?' she said. He raised an eyebrow, and she told him its name. He remembered it, had watched it years ago with a long-forgotten girlfriend. The sort of film where nothing much happens. A young, attractive couple meet by chance in Vienna, and spend the day wandering around the city, talking and getting to know each other. There had been a sequel too, he thought.

It was March, and Western Europe was battered by storms. Dan had been due to fly back from Madrid to London that afternoon. He had checked the weather forecast that morning and had travelled to the airport knowing full well that no planes would be flying out that day. There was nothing else he could have done, as the airline had not cancelled his flight. Instead, the departures board merely announced a one-hour delay.

Dan sighed, briefly considered - and rejected - the option of a cappuccino at Starbucks, and strode to the nearest bar, where he ordered a gin and tonic. He took a sip, then began checking his work emails.

As he sat frowning at his phone, a young woman came up to the bar, ordered a drink and sat down on his right. He noticed her book before he noticed her: Albert Camus, *La Peste*, in the original French. Yet the girl herself was not French; she had ordered her glass of Rioja in a flat, Midlands accent.

He stole a look at her, then another. The third time he was caught; her eyes met his, and she smiled. He smiled back, gesturing at the Camus.

'Great book,' he said, 'although I've only read it in translation.'

'Me too, up until now,' she replied. 'But I don't get much chance to speak French these days. I need the practice, otherwise I'll forget everything.'

He laughed. 'Tell me about it! I studied French at

university, and I can barely ask for a beer these days. And it's more or less the same word!'

Her face was all angles, with slanting cheekbones, and her eyes a pale, luminous green. Her mouth was wide, almost comically so, and slightly turned up at the corners. 'Like a duck,' she said, with a self-deprecating laugh; she had been nicknamed Duckface at school. The turned-up ends made her look as if she were permanently smiling; the effect was more attractive than she realised.

He held out his hand. 'I'm Dan,' he said.

'Kate.' Her hands were small and delicate, yet her grip was surprisingly firm.

She was twenty-seven – 'twenty-eight next week' - and had left university three years earlier with a degree in Modern Languages. Keen for adventure, she had eschewed the career paths chosen by most of her peers - postgraduate degrees, teacher training college or graduate training schemes - and had taken the ten-week course that enabled her to teach English as a foreign language. She lived in Prague, where she worked in a language school in the Old Town. She had been visiting a friend from university in a town around 70 miles from Madrid.

He was three years older, and had also studied languages, although his interest in the subject had waned early. He had taken a second degree in law, trained as a solicitor, and worked for one of the larger City firms, specialising in construction law. 'It's even less interesting than it sounds,' he said with a wry smile. He was in town for a conference, which had finished the previous day. It was his first visit to Madrid, and he had decided to stay an extra day to explore the city.

'Well,' said Kate, 'I might just check the departures board and see what they're saying about my flight.' She laughed. 'Ridiculous, isn't it? We all know that nobody's flying anywhere this afternoon!'

She came back to report that the departures board was still showing a distinct lack of candour; both flights had been delayed by a further hour.

Dan made a face. 'Oh well, you'd better have another glass of wine. I'll join you.' He gestured to the barman and ordered two glasses of Rioja. By this time, the bar was getting busy, so they decamped to a small table in the corner.

He learned about her childhood growing up in Nottingham, her mother's death when she was only thirteen, the stepmother her father had married barely a year later. It was strange; she was not usually one to overshare, and she had known him all of thirty minutes. But there was something about him that inspired confidences. He would have made a good therapist, she thought. In turn, he described the small town in Kent where he had grown up, how stifling it was, and how glad he had been to escape it.

As they talked, they became aware of a commotion outside - people complaining, raised voices, the odd curse. Dan went to investigate; the departures board had finally admitted the truth, and all flights for the rest of the day had been cancelled.

They finished their drinks and went to the airline desk - they had booked with the same airline. The storm was expected to blow itself out by morning, and their flights had been rescheduled for the following afternoon. Overnight accommodation and meals would be provided at an airport hotel; they were given vouchers and directed to a waiting coach.

'Well,' said Dan, while they waited at reception to collect their keys, 'I don't know about you, but I'm not going to spend the evening watching TV in a hotel room. We have an extra day in Madrid; might as well use it. Shall we go into town, have a walk around, then find somewhere for dinner?'

They took a taxi to the Old Town and wandered round the maze of narrow streets around the Plaza Major. Despite the wind and rain, the square was busy with tourists. They stopped at a toyshop and Dan bought a little stuffed giraffe. 'For my nephew,' he explained, 'my sister Lucy's baby. He'll be six months old next week.' He took out his phone and showed her a photo of a solemn-looking infant with a pudgy face. In the little jewellery shop next door, she exclaimed over a little silver pendant in the shape of a star, which he insisted on buying for her. 'For your birthday,' he said when she protested, 'since I won't see you.'

They stopped at a sherry bar and drank a Fino each, then moved on to another bar, where they ordered tapas and a bottle of Rioja. They sat at a table in a dark corner, surrounded on three sides by wine casks. She told him of her life in Prague, the English school in the Old Town, her circle of friends. They were mostly language graduates like herself, seeking adventure and romance before settling down to a career, mortgage and family life. They were a close-knit bunch, with their little cliques, feuds and casual romances. She did not mention her growing disenchantment, her slow realisation that she was merely extending her student life in order to put off the chore of growing up. In turn he talked about his life in London - long hours at work, until 9.00 pm or even 10.00 pm some nights, then home to his tiny flat. It had to be done; he was up for partnership next year, and competition was fierce. He liked living alone, he said, could never go back to the flat shares of his student days. And yet it could be lonely, going home to an empty flat. 'So,' she said, after a pause, 'How come a handsome lawyer like yourself doesn't have a girlfriend?'

He smiled ruefully, looked away, was silent for a moment. 'I was engaged once. But, well … there was someone else. For her, I mean. Another man. Since then,' he shrugged. 'It's difficult to trust, you know?'

She smiled in sympathy. 'Me too, actually. Not engaged, but we were together for five years.'

He reached across the narrow table and briefly touched her hand. 'He must have been an idiot to cheat on you.'

Once dinner was over, they left the restaurant and wandered further along the street away from the Plaza, until eventually they came to a bar. The crowd was younger and more stylishly dressed than in the tourist bars around the Plaza Major. They were mainly locals, and there were no English voices other than their own. There was a balcony running the length of the room, overlooking the street, but it was still raining, so they took the last free table inside, in a far corner. A waitress came over to take their order, and for some reason, they both chose elaborate fruity cocktails with preposterous names. They felt as if they were on a summer holiday, despite the weather.

Their conversation had moved onto politics, and they were relieved to find that their opinions more or less matched. They eventually found a topic on which they disagreed, and each defended his or her opinion robustly. 'Is this our first fight?' Dan asked with a mock frown, causing Kate to collapse into giggles.

By then, the bar was getting busier. A DJ was setting up, and they saw that their table was on the edge of a small dance floor. Presently, he started playing, and to their relief they heard, not the doof doof doof of the clubs they no longer frequented, but cheesy pop hits, the sort you would hear at a wedding disco. And the crowd, young, hip, and glamorous, seemed to be lapping it up; the dance floor was filling up quickly.

'Bit old for this, aren't we?' Dan shouted above the din. Kate laughed.

'Come on, Grandad, you're not quite pension age yet.'

A song came on that they both remembered from their teenage years. Emboldened by the sherry, wine and cocktails, Kate grabbed Dan's hand and pulled him onto the tiny dance floor.

After a while, hot and tired from dancing, they went out onto the balcony into the cool air. It had finally stopped raining. He turned to face her, reached up and tucked a loose strand of hair behind her ear. Then he slid his arms around her waist and pulled her towards him.

In his room in the sterile hotel, they shared an illicit cigarette on the balcony, each wrapped in a sheet. A guilty pleasure for them both; they had both taken up smoking at university in an effort to look cool, but had long since given up, other than the odd lapse.

'So, your fiancée - how long has it been?' she asked, a little shyly.

'Eighteen months.'

'And no-one since then?'

'Not really. I'm not really the one-night stand sort.' He looked down at the sheet and laughed. 'Believe it or not! What about you and your boyfriend?'

'Three years.'

'And no one for you? No one at all?'

'Not really. There was someone, for a couple of months, but it fizzled out. It was soon after Jack and I split up, and I don't think I was ready.'

'You don't strike me as the sort of person who goes in for one-night stands either.' He laughed again. 'Yet here we are!' The next morning, they sat at breakfast across from each other, sharing the same English newspaper, like an old married couple. The storm had abated, and the weather was calm once more; their flights would be leaving as scheduled. Kate's flight was due to leave first, and Dan's a couple of hours later. He came with her to the departure gate and waited with her in the café. He looked at his watch; 23 hours and 42 minutes since he had sat down at the bar and ordered his gin and tonic. They sat with their cafes con leche in silence, suddenly shy; for all the intimacy of the previous evening, they were virtual strangers, after all. The whole time they had been sitting there, sipping their coffees, Kate had been sending him quick little glances; would she, dare she, speak? Was he thinking it too? Presently her flight was called, and they stood up.

'So, listen,' she said, trying to keep the nervousness out of her voice. 'I come here every few months to visit Clare. I'll be coming again in September. What if ... I mean, do you want to meet up again?'

'Seriously? Just like in the film, you mean?'

'Why not?' Her face was turned up towards him, smiling hopefully; she looked like a young child.

He hesitated, then his face slowly broke into a smile.

'OK,' he said, 'Why not? Let's do it!'

They took out their phones, looked at calendars, suggested dates. They settled on a day in the middle of the month, a Saturday.

'Where shall we meet?'

He thought. 'The sherry cafe we went to yesterday? No, scrap that, I'm not sure I could find it again. Better play it safe - the Square itself? The statue in the middle?'

It was agreed; the Plaza Major, Saturday 17 September at 3.00 pm. They grinned at each other, giddy with excitement at what they had just done.

Her flight was called again, last call. Or rather, last

and final call, that bizarre phrase which is only ever heard in airports. As if 'last' on its own might be open to misinterpretation.

He slid his arms around her waist and pulled her close, just as he had done the previous night. 'Until September.'

'Until September,' she whispered back.

He stood watching her, straight and slender, as she passed through the double doors and disappeared.

She arrives at her small flat around 9.30 pm. Her flatmate, another English teacher, is out, probably staying with her boyfriend. She makes herself a cup of herbal tea and sits by the window to drink it. Her flat is near the castle, and the whole city is laid out before her. It was the view that had made her choose this flat. For the same money, she could have rented somewhere larger in a less sought-after area. But it is worth it, just to wake up every morning to that view.

She yawns; she did not get much sleep last night, and the reason for this makes her blush, even though she is alone. She brushes her teeth, puts on an old T-shirt, and climbs into her narrow bed.

As she lies there, she replays the previous evening in her mind. She pictures herself in six months' time getting on the flight, standing in the Plaza Major next to the statue, waiting for him. It is impossible, a fantasy, a pipe dream. He will have forgotten her by next week. And yet ... she falls asleep thinking of him, a smile playing across her mouth.

He lets himself into the silent flat. 11.10 pm; he really should go straight to bed. He has been out of the office for an extra day, and tomorrow will be especially busy. But he does not feel tired yet, and knows that if he goes to bed now, he will not sleep.

He goes to the drinks cabinet, pours himself a large

whisky and sits down in his favourite armchair. There is
a lamp next to the chair, but he leaves it unlit. There is a
streetlamp outside, and he sits in the half-light, thinking
of nothing in particular, just letting his thoughts wash over
him.

There is a sound from behind him. She stands in the
doorway, squinting in the gloom.

'Hello! Why are you sitting in the dark?'

She crosses the room, sits down on the arm of his chair,
and runs her fingers through his hair. He slips an arm
round her waist, reaches up to kiss her.

'How's he been?'

'A bit unsettled - went down at seven, and he's had me
up twice already. I think he might have a tooth coming
through - he's the right age for it.'

He reaches up to tuck a loose strand of her hair round
her ear. 'You go back to bed, then. I'll be through in a
minute.'

He finishes his whisky, rises, and walks to the kitchen
to rinse out his glass. He takes his washbag out of his case
but leaves the case itself in the hallway - no need to unpack
tonight. He brushes his teeth and gets undressed.

The door to the nursery is ajar, and there is a faint glow
from the nightlight by the cot. He stands for a minute,
looking down at his sleeping child. He remembers the
stuffed giraffe in his case; he will present it tomorrow, and
he pictures his son's delight, the fat little dimpled hands
reaching for it. He repositions a stray bunny, strokes his
son's fuzzy head, then slips out quietly. The sight of his
bare left hand reminds him there is one last thing to do
before he goes to bed; going back into the hall, he takes his
wedding ring from an inside pocket of his case and replaces
it on his finger.

He crosses the hall to the master bedroom and gets into

bed next to his wife. She stirs slightly, mutters something unintelligible, settles back to sleep. He slides an arm round her and nestles in beside her sleeping form. For a fleeting moment, an image from the previous night flashes across his consciousness. Then his mind empties of all thought, and he slips into an untroubled sleep.

Fountains In Paris

Beth Steiner

Beth is a doctor of theology and mythology, seaside-lover and occasional clutz, working in academic research development. She loves science fiction TV, live music, and her garden, and she exercises as much as she can except on pub night. Beth also likes to 'try to make a difference' at a fairly low busybody level. Her poetry has been published in various journals.

Light fronds of sweetened stone
writhe like ribbons
as they climb the air
around their precious water.
The young and the gorgeous
dance in the pools,
shimmering in the sun like ripples.

Wishing for peace
in white wine and smouldering cigarettes,
I found my most beautiful time.
The sweetness and excitement
of whistling seventeen,
I learned,
is found in large hats on balconies.

The whole city smells yellow,
not the gold of the stars
in those drops of bounding water,
nor the musky bronze
of every church I could not pass by.

Flickering within streams of colour
your songs of summer remind me
that all we need in life
are magnificent distractions.

Baklava And Umm Haram

Erini Loucaides

Erini Loucaides is an Australian-Cypriot writer with a BA in English from the University of London. Her writing has been shortlisted by Bridport 2020, Fresher 2018, and Sydney Morning Herald 1988;. Her work has been featured in the Fresher Anthology, 100 Words of Solitude, Cadences Literary Journal, RSL's Only Connect and Mslexia. She was selected by the Commonwealth Foundation for a 2020 summer mentorship with Jennifer Makumbi.

Cypriot coffee is an orgasm on its precipice, the tantric
sex of brewing: stirring, rising, pulling back, heating
up, pausing, waiting, rising once more, then pouring as
it bubbles up. It needs patience, needs to be watched.
There are occasions when she has turned her attention to
Viber messages and the *mbrikki* has overflowed, caffeine
graffitiing her stove and benchtop like old blood.

Right now, she is focused on the coffee, stirring its grainy
texture, releasing its old-soil-and-roasted-chestnut smell.
Her phone is on silent, new messages hidden. She thinks.
She checks again, just in case, because he's here, sitting in
the tapestry armchair, reading the newspaper waiting for
his afternoon brew. Once, the screen had flashed green and
the grrrr of the phone had vibrated against the wooden
benchtop. That had sent her heart galloping. She'd cursed
herself for forgetting, for not double checking. Thankfully,
he'd been close to the TV and hadn't heard the vibration.

What would he do if he found out, she often wonders.
Much like falling off a bolting horse. It would break his
metaphorical back. Fragment his Cypriot pride. But then
he'd piece most of it back together and that's when he'd
probably tie her to the back of a horse and have it drag
her through his mother's village, or maybe tie her to the
festering palm tree outside, slather her in honey, sit back
with his coffee and watch as the wasps attacked.

As the coffee begins to brew, puffing up like dark
lava, she can't help but return to thoughts of how
her husband hasn't a clue about slow rising, stirring,
simmering, pausing, watching, pulling back, heating up.
His lovemaking is a Cypriot coffee left unattended – quick
boil and spill. Lately, it's worse. After the flesh flapping of
sex, he rolls away, snoring soon graffitiing the bedroom.
Sometimes he dreams of his lost lands and mumbles, 'A
good Turk is a dead Turk'. She has stopped pushing his

65

shoulders in his half-sleep, stopped trying to shake the foulness out of his mouth. These days she just tip toes downstairs and checks for any new hidden Viber messages.

There are many other things she has had to learn since moving from London to Cyprus five years ago. She sometimes thinks of herself as an English tea bag steeped in hot Cypriot water.

The first time she'd visited the village of Pyla, about two years ago, a local woman had called out from her stall, there where bric a brac and food were on sale.

Buy jisveh, nice coffee pot, I will give you very good price.

Her English ear couldn't tell the seller's accent was Turkish-tinged, nor had she known that Pyla was one of the very few villages on the island where Turkish and Greek Cypriots lived together. She'd bought the little bronze pot knowing how Nikos loved his coffee. That afternoon, she'd proudly waved it at him, flag-like.

Coffee with kaimaki coming up in your new jisveh.
Mbrikki, woman. That is a mbrikki. Always.

But the lady in Pyla called it jisveh.

Madeleine, what were you doing in Pyla? Buying from a barbaric Ottoman, a relic who refused to move her old fat ass to Turkey? Don't ever call it jisveh and don't ever buy anything from a Turk, you hear? Not while under my roof. Get that fucking thing out of my house.

She did not tell him how the seller was neither old nor fat, nor how gracious she was, gifting her with a stubby broom that was more of an uprooted thyme bush. For the *creepy crawlies*, the lady had smiled.

Yeah, for my husband's centipede sentences.

There'd also been Ahmet and his handsome son, Mustafa. They'd generously served up tahini buns and semolina cakes. In fact, all the stall sellers had been so warm, so open.

The coffee is now thickening into that velvety top layer they prize so much here, the kaimaki. She scoops it off the stove and carefully pours it in the porcelain demi-tasse. She skirts past the kitchen table, the sofa, and places the coffee on the footstool next to him. The sun is hazily filtering in through the beige, gauzy curtains (hideous wedding gift from his mother). She'd love to throw them open and let the full brilliance of the afternoon sun enter the living room but she knows it'll froth up an argument. And Madeleine needs him quiet now, immersed in his newspaper. She needs him on silent. But he breaks it with a command.

'Bring me a baklava.'

She tries not to show her chagrin as she heads to the fridge and takes out the Tupperware his mother fills with a week's worth of baklava. Her husband refuses to believe 'baklava' is a Turkish word despite her showing him various internet sites tracing the word's etymology. *'It's Greek, stolen by the savages, like everything else. Do your research properly.'* She should have known that would be his answer.

The knife in her hand makes an elaborate act of separating the sticky rhombus sweets, but at some point, her fingers flee to the phone beside the Tupperware. Tap. Tap. Tap. New Viber message.

Be there in 40.

She deletes it immediately. Never safe to savour. Never risk storing a message to warmly re-read. She saves them inside her instead.

As she slides a baklava piece onto a plate, she says as casually as she can, 'I'm going for a coffee with Elena and Suzanne in a bit.'

'Where to?' he looks up briefly. Is it her imagination or is his black moustache twitching?

'One of the cafes along the seafront, probably Nero, if there's space. Gets so packed in there.'

She needs to create uncertainty, say nothing definite that could then be questioned. She decides to cover herself a little more.

'And I might pop into Meneou village afterwards. We need fruit and veg. That new market is making a killing.'

'I don't see why you can't support Michalis here in our neighbourhood.'

'Your cousin better get his act together if he doesn't want to lose more customers. Old cabbage, banged up apples. Never has any sweet potatoes but always promises he'll bring some.'

He grumbles under his breath about how embarrassing it'll look if word gets out that his wife is shopping elsewhere.

She steals a glance at the Ikea clock on the wall rather than her phone. Time feels stuck solid, baklava time. Phone in jean pocket, she makes her way upstairs, moments of uncertainty striking her as she climbs each step to the bedroom. It soon disperses when the nozzle is turned on. The warm water splashes on her splayed fingers for a few, open moments until his voice booms up the stairs. Her jeans and underwear are pooled at her ankles and T-shirt is hanging off one shoulder as she hollers back down.

'What did you say?'

'I said, for God sake's woman, baklava doesn't need a fridge.'

'Your mother told me to refrigerate it when the weather gets warmer so the nuts don't spoil.'

'Then use your brains and let it thaw. I feel like I'm crunching on fucking dinosaur teeth.'

Don't answer, Maddy, she commands herself, heading back to the shower. *Let him turn himself off. Stay quiet if you're going to get out on time and unfrazzled.*

Her showering is quick, manic almost. As she dries herself, she stares at her wardrobe and wonders what would she wear if she were meeting the girls for coffee. Darker jeans and a cotton top, navy striped. Sorted. Hair: quick brush down. Her long thin blonde hair is easy to brush anyway. Make up: a smudge of eyeliner, no shadow and a light dab of coral lipstick. Perfume? That she'll put on when she's in the car. The little glass bottle is in her handbag. Easier that way.

She's not quite descended the stairs when he gestures with his chin at the cup and saucer on the footstool. 'Put these in the sink before you go.'

She obliges then grabs the keys from the counter. Her heart begins to canter. 'I'm off.'

'Be back in an hour.' He doesn't glance up.

Before she closes the front door, she catches her husband's profile in the lowering sun. It's only in this rugged side view that Madeleine still sees echoes of the man she fell in love with. His profile is a wild, Cypriot landscape with its cliffs and shores, promontory lips. She had so loved exploring it, especially when they used to ride on his motorbike (now sold), along the palm tree promenade, giddy arms around him, her windswept face gazing up at his, inhaling the fabric softener of his T-shirt. When she stops seeing and smelling these echoes, that's when she'll probably leave.

Five minutes later, she is rolling down Larnaca's arteries realising that she actually has some time to kill. Her driving slows, meandering into narrow side streets. No matter how many times she drives through them, these street names here still fascinate her: *Mehmet Ali*, *Istanbul* and *Zehra*. Further down, to the right, is the old Turkish-Cypriot cemetery. Adjacent to it, are the retired boats belonging to Greek-Cypriot fishermen. The wooden bones of *Ayios Nikolaos* and *Princess Christina* lie a stone's throw from the buried bones of *Yousouf Sayegh* and *Mahasseen Ramaly*.

Much as her husband would like to bury them, the Ottoman layers are here, stuck like baklava pastry, glued by the syrup of history.

Madeleine thinks of Suzanne, her long-time buddy, who gave up her life in Sydney to marry Bambos. Suzanne's words often ring in her ear, Aussie accent as pronounced as the freckles on her skin.

We Anglos have been living on Aboriginal land for the same amount of time as Turkish-Cypriots have been here. D'ya reckon we oughtta shove off back to England now?

She used to try telling her husband this, but all he would spit out was: *Turks, Turkish-Cypriots, same dog blood.*

Suddenly her phone lights up. Vibrates. Grrrr.

Nearly there.

Read and delete. She drives on, to another Ottoman layer. A place Nikos can never know she visits.

The Salt Lake is cracked with dirty whiteness, the flamingos have gone. She curves around the lake, eerie in its late Spring dryness. Scattered couples are taking selfies as the sun flares its glorious yellows and reds. But Madeleine cannot stop and admire now. She drives deeper into the cluster of giant palms, cypresses and carobs, into the Muslim world's third most revered temple.

Hala Sultan Tekke.

Even though Hellenic Bronze Age layers have been unearthed, it is still a place of worship for Muslims. That is reason enough to never set foot here, according to her husband. Ottoman stamping upon Hellenic. But for Madeleine, it is a soft and feminine place, partly because of the curly ornate gates at the entrance, the rose gardens inside, the arches and cream domes, the soft rugs inside the temple that one must walk barefoot upon.

But it's feminine mainly because of Umm Haram. Tekke temple is a shrine to prophet Mohammed's aunt. Her bones are here, under a metre-high mausoleum draped in emerald silk, embroidered with gold stars and moons.

Umm Haram. Madeleine loves her name. It could inspire classical compositions, poems. Perhaps it has. *Umm Haram: Prelude in E minor violin. Ode to Umm Haram.*

This place has cradled Madeleine many times. Here she has come when jobs and foetuses were lost. Now though, she comes for another reason.

On this late afternoon, there are no tourists, no Turkish-Cypriots on a pilgrimage, no maintenance men. Only the usual band of stray cats which aren't actually stray. She pulls over behind an unruly carob and switches the car engine off. She scans the woods ahead, along the dirt trail of palms and pines and cypresses, where it is said Umm Haram met her death, thrown off her startled horse.

You were a devout, faithful wife. You came all the way from Arabia with your husband and here's what you got soon after. Knocked off by a horse. Ended up a pile of mangled bones under dirty hooves.

Sometimes, especially at twilight, Madeleine feels as if Umm Haram is there, between the trees, still on her horse, veiled eyes watching her.

The next vibration startles her. She fumbles for her phone, reads the message. Smiles. Deletes. Then, out of the red leather handbag, she takes a glass bottle. She shakes it between thumb and forefinger, uncorks it, and with the tip of her forefinger, dabs 'Shalimar' on her throat, her wrists. The voluptuous scent of bergamot, iris and jasmine fills the car. Madeleine smells her skin as a lover might.

The cats inside the temple garden, near the roses, have

stopped licking themselves and are now staring at her like furry gargoyles. Their slitty eyes watch her movements as she dabs more perfume between her breasts.

Bad girl, putting on your Shalimar, just like the slutty 1920s flappers did. Bad, bad girl, we know what you've been up to and we're going to tell Umm Haram.

Fuck you, bitches, she whispers to them, *get back to licking your arses.*

She drives away from the temple entrance and into the woods, all the while peering through her rear-view mirror until she sees the car behind her. Its number plates are two-lettered, in a bolder black than those here in the south of Cyprus, with a custard yellow background. The vehicle may look out of place anywhere else in Cyprus but not here in Tekke.

They park their cars in in different areas of the woods and walk towards the densest part, where the dark green branches of one tree merge with the next.

Time is honey unspun. The woods are heavy with the scent of the cypresses' spicy earthiness.

They find each other between the prostate trees. Madeleine gazes into carob eyes, into expressions, that, at thirty-nine (thirsty nine, she has half-jokingly taken to calling it), she thought she was too old for.

Emine, slightly taller, heavier, draws her close. She caresses Madeleine's left cheek. Madeleine can smell the cloves Emine likes to spice her desserts with. Her lover's eyes are mahogany suns, her smile as warm as it was the day she had sold the *jisveh* to her at the Pyla market stalls.

Madeleine reaches up, twines her fingers around a lock of Emine's curly hair, the auburn tints glowing in the sinking sun.

Emine's voice, warm as a log fire, heavy with accent, fills the spaces between the cypress leaves.

'Madeleine, there is another spot that I think will work, much safer than here. The back of Oroklini village.'

'It's too far out, Emmy. The drive will take too long. It'll mean less time together. Let's keep meeting here for now, it's the only place that can explain why you're here. I know it troubles you, it being your religious temple and all but . . .'

Emine nods, furrows her dark brows, but the temple behind them is soon forgotten. Emine takes Madeleine's face into her hands.

Their kiss begins as tame as the rose garden nearby, embroidered with gold stars and moons, but soon the kiss gathers force, wild and galloping in its forbiddenness.

And Umm Haram is flung from her horse once more.

The Other Side

Vyv Nugent

Vyv is an unpublished writer of poetry, short stories and one novel. His writing varies widely in content and style, but broadly centres on his unique perspective on his home planet, its colourful inhabitants, and their countless frailties. He currently lives with his wife, dog and cat in a quiet coastal village in West Wales, where he especially enjoys walking the rugged Pembrokeshire cliffs, growing good things to eat, and then eating them.

At the start, when they first met, the way ahead was so
unclear,
although his heart missed many beats, his careful head
could not decide,
and so, she smiled, held his hand, and whispered softly in
his ear,
'I'll see you round the second bend, and on the other side.'

In the weeks and months that drifted by, he opened his
heart,
he told her all his hopes and fears, and of the love he'd been
denied,
and when she saw his spirit broken, and his world so torn
apart,
she said, 'I'll wait around the second bend, and on the other
side.'

And so, his life became much easier with every passing day,
and every night they held each other, and in each they
would confide,
and then before she fell asleep, she would hold onto him
and say,
'I'll see you round the second bend, and on the other side.'

One night, beside a moonlit stream, he gazed into her
smile,
and said, 'I love you more than life itself, and even more
beside,'
and so, she jumped up, and she skipped away, and laughing
all the while,
she cried, 'You'll find me round the second bend, and on the
other side.'

Within a week he asked of her what needed to be said,

and on a sunny autumn afternoon he took her for his bride,
and just before the vows were read, she smiled and
squeezed his hand,
and said, 'I'll see you round the second bend, and on the
other side.'

Then on a winter's night he found a lump, not seen before,
and so, she nursed and reassured him, and she took it in
her stride,
and then she got him through the worst of it, and through
the open door,
there to negotiate the second bend, and find the other side.

So soon the months turned into years, the decades they ran
free,
and they loved each other deeply, without end, without
divide,
and they watched each other change, and wondered how
their lives
would come to be, just around the second bend, and on the
other side.

And now they've reached their passing, and the way ahead
is clear,
soon their lights they will have faded, and their bodies will
have died, but then,
she somehow finds the strength to smile, and whisper softly
in his ear...
'I'll see you round the second bend, and on the other side.'

Johannesburg

Joe Bedford

Joe Bedford is a writer from Doncaster, UK. His short stories have been published widely, including in Litro, Structo and the Mechanics' Institute Review, and are available to read at joebedford.co.uk. He can be contacted via Twitter at @ joebedford_uk.

It was me who insisted we travel by rail. Rhodes tried to laugh off the idea, since it tripled the length and cost of our trip, but in the end I simply refused to take a flight, and he walked off while I was explaining the absurdity of taking a budget airline to a conference on organic farming. Now, with the conference behind us, the fact that we're stuck together on this train for the next thirty-six hours sits heavy in my stomach.

As we pull out of Johannesburg, he unpacks a few things in silence and slams the cabin door on the way out. Maybe he'll manage to sulk all the way to Cape Town.The conference hosted speakers from all over the world. At first, Rhodes made a point of asking delegates how they'd got to Johannesburg, and then saying: 'Naturally. Good flight?' But after a beer he seemed to enjoy mingling with the farmers. He was lively and candid, and stood out from the start. Most of the delegates were well-spoken and zealous about the environment. All of them but me were white. Rhodes showed no embarrassment explaining that we paid for New Promise Farm with the money he makes restoring motorbikes. I had to stop him forcing a group of Americans to look at pictures of his Harley. I heard him tell someone the farm would run him into the ground. When he noticed I'd heard him, he just shrugged. Running New Promise has been difficult, it's true. It's a sandy tract of land overgrown with invasive Port Jackson willow which we're still clearing after three years. We pump water from a borehole and store it in ferrocement tanks. Our beds produce just enough vegetables to feed ourselves and our son Dion, and to keep a small stall at a farmers' market. But without Rhodes's business we'd have nothing at all.

He won't admit it, but this one inescapable fact underlies every discussion we've ever had about the farm. It surfaces constantly in the form of sighs, grunts, glances. Despite the fact I run the farm by myself, the look in Rhodes's eye when I bring him an unexpected outgoing   that he sees me, ultimately, as a frittering housewife.

Even if I am the one with the dirt under their nails. The cabin door opens but I ignore it. The sun is high over Gauteng. My stomach turns as he sits down.

'Sorry,' he says. I worry he's going to make his apologies now, before I'm prepared. 'It's Opa.'

His father – an old-fashioned Afrikaner who raised Rhodes on an intensive farm, since lost.

'He wants to know whether the compost can be turned.'

All through the weekend, Rhodes has been texting his parents back and forth as they watch the farm. Their questions have been mostly banal – some so banal that I can sense their scepticism of my methods, as if I were trying to heave up every basic fundament of agriculture. They've directed all their questions to Rhodes, who knows nothing about the farm and so has deferred to me every single time.

The only question they texted me directly was where I kept the detergent.

I explain about the compost without looking away from the window. I know he's noticed my nervous breathing. Fuck him for putting me in this position. Everything within me wants to get out of the cabin. Then he jumps up, mumbles another apology and leaves.

My heart beats furiously inside my chest. A flash of misery runs through me.

Yes. Maybe this is the end. There's nothing to do on this train – I spend the whole day staring out of the window. And now the light is failing and I'm thinking of my parents.

They lived happily together right up until my mother's death. My father went soon after, complicit with his illness and eager to follow her. Their relationship was difficult

– my father white English, my mother Cape Coloured.
My father's father disowned him, and my mother faced
prejudice throughout her life. Regardless, they worked
hard and moved up quickly. Their relationship with
Rhodes'sparents, who they met infrequently in the last
years of their life, never really extended beyond formalities.
Their accord was quiet and polite and nothing more.

When Rhodes and I married, few people took exception
– only Rhodes's most distant cousins questioned my
heritage. Dion was born into a happy family. Then we took
the farm. We coasted for about a year on the excitement of
the purchase, working all hours to clear the land, while I
read widely and led the designs. We chatted long into the
dark country nights, over bonfires of Port Jackson. But the
first summer scorched our beds and split our tank. From
then on, the hitches hammered at us from every side. By
the time Dion started school, Rhodes and I were sleeping in
separate beds.

We hadn't slept together since, until four nights ago in a
single-bedded cabin identical to this one, on the way to the
conference. We'd actually been happy that night, leaving
New Promise behind us.

The prospect of sharing a bed with him after what
happened in Johannesburg horrifies me. But where else is
he supposed to sleep tonight?

Rehearsals of the argument we're going to have muddy
up my head.

It's just too much.The train is long and full – I find
Rhodes towards the back. Judging by the men sat on the
floor by the carriage door, I guess he's paid someone to take
their seat. He's snoring with his mouth open, the only white
person in the carriage.

The argument I'd rehearsed dissolves into wasted
emotion. I consider taking the bottle cradled in the crook of

his arm, as I'd done on Friday night when Yusuf – our host in Johannesburg – found him unconscious in the garage. Christ, I want to shout at him. But I think better of it. Instead, I march back and shut myself in the cabin.

Outside, the countryside is black and empty. Somewhere, farmers are bedding down, bushmen are drinking and laughing. Dion will already be in bed.

I force out a few useless tears, and sleep.I wake with a start. Rhodes is sitting under the window. The train is stationary, the engine running. I pull the covers up over my body.

'We're at Kimberley,' he says. 'About 45 minutes.'

I rub my eyes. 'What do you want?'

Normally, a snap like this would provoke an argument. He seems to consider one.

'Text from Opa.' His voice is flat. 'The pump's lost pressure.'

I give the instructions bitterly. My phone rings.

'Is it my mother?' he asks while texting.

My throat tightens. 'No.'

I try to put the phone down as if I'm already thinking of something else but he's looking right at me.

He knows. 'Well?'

I stare out at Kimberley Station, but too much time has passed. He'll only ask again.

'It was Yusuf.'

I hold his gaze for the first time since Johannesburg. He's the one to break it.

'So what does he want?'

He wants to apologise for not being there for me on Sunday.

'I don't know, I didn't answer it.'

Now there'll be a fight. I watch him fetch 50 rand from his suitcase and then, without a word, walk to the door.

He pauses there and for a moment an old instinct of pity tries to make me say something but I hold my tongue. Poor stupid man.

The door clicks shut and the train pulls out of Kimberley.

It was never a secret that Rhodes hated Yusuf. It had nothing to do with the fact that Yusuf and I fooled around at university, but more to do with some fundamental rivalry that I will never understand.

Yusuf is disliked by most average South Africans. He wears tie-dye and sandals and lets his hair grow long and uncombed. His business card lists 'Freelance Consultant' – his usual work – underneath 'Free Spirit'. Typically, his conversation turns quickly to veganism, ley lines, conspiracy theories, his amalgam of religious beliefs. What he rarely mentions is his given name – George – or his divorce or the twin girls she took with her, whom he never gets to see.

He was keen to put us up for the conference. When in Johannesburg, he stays in a gated community in Sandton which Rhodes always reminds me was inherited from his grandparents. Though that's always whispered. Rhodes was relieved that the talks kept him tied up for most of the weekend. So it was only in the evenings that tensions were allowed to flare.

Friday night passed smoothly. We'd just arrived and Yusuf threw a party for the delegation. When Rhodes passed out in the garage, Yusuf proclaimed a personal victory against alcohol that my husband was too drunk to remember. But on Saturday, when the three of us sat alone at Yusuf's dining table, I knew instinctively that there would be an argument.

Conversation was slow at first, mostly around the conference. When Yusuf diverted it towards extra terrestrial life, Rhodes ate in complete silence until the subject passed.

I was bored by the adolescent tension coming from my husband, so I introduced a topic I knew we'd all agree on.

'Springboks are looking good this year.'

Rhodes picked up immediately. Even Yusuf, who'd systematically tried to shed his links with 'George', couldn't resist the schoolyard excitement of rugby. We stayed on course right through dessert, until Rhodes said in passing: 'Should get Dion into the school team.'

The slight lull that followed was noticeably protracted. Rhodes was suspicious – he thought he'd said something innocuous.

Yusuf took the initiative. It was in the wrong direction.

'You know my feelings on the school system. I'm still trying to get the twins out of there.'

Yusuf had homeschooled his daughters until they were taken away, something we had been talking about extensively over the phone. Maybe I shouldn't have, but I kept these calls from Rhodes, knowing it would be easier to open the debate if I'd made up my own mind first. I didn't realise until then that I already had.

'School is crucial at that age,' said Rhodes. 'It's where you learn about the world.'

'Exactly.' Yusuf became smug. 'Laws, punishments, competition, conformity.'

Rhodes's voice rose as he counted on his fingers. 'Education. Your mates. Sense of responsibility.'

The pair spoke over each other until Rhodes tried to bring me into it.

'We spoke about it briefly before, didn't we?'

'Yes. Briefly.'

Another awkward silence. Rhodes asked if I'd been thinking about it. I told him I had.

'For Dion?'

'Of course for Dion!'

He seemed genuinely surprised. I explained my recent feelings about Dion's school, feelings I'd only so far discussed with Yusuf. I told him I was confident I could school Dion myself while maintaining the farm.

'This is unbelievable,' said Rhodes, and I wasn't surprised.

I thought for a moment he was going to square off to Yusuf, who seemed suddenly desperate to leave the table. Instead it was Rhodes who got up and left. He took a taxi into the city and arrived back at midnight. I assumed by his quietness that he wanted to drop the subject until we got back to New Promise. I conceded.

We slept in the twins' room, laid flat on their separate single beds, surrounded by the drawings and exercises of their homeschooling, marked in red by their father.

I'm half-asleep when Rhodes returns to the cabin. It's noon, which means we're only a few hours from Cape Town. The fact that he's slumped into his seat tells me that he plans on staying put for the rest of the journey. Fine. So let him sulk.

Awkward silences, though painful, have long since been the norm. So I'm stunned to hear his voice.

'We have to talk about Dion.'

Christ. Is this it then? Is one of us finally going to broach the D-word? Or does he want to have the conversation he tried to start on Sunday, in the final hours of the conference, the conversation we can never go back from? I straighten up.

'You want to talk about homeschooling?' I say. 'Now? You're pathetic.'

The bitterness spurs me on. He takes it painlessly.

'I don't want it discussed in front of him,' he says. Pathetic.

85

'Well, of course not, Rhodes. Who in their right mind would ask their child what they wanted?'

'That's not what I mean.'

'If you want to talk, go ahead. I'll just sit here.'

'That's unfair.'

'Unfair?' I'm losing control of the situation. 'You're ridiculous.'

The memory of Sunday afternoon is rushing to my head – the hush in the conference room, the eyes of the delegates.

'Look,' he says, 'We can talk about Sunday when we––'

The train is suddenly hot and dizzying. Outside I see the vineyards of the Western Cape glow yellow. Loud, open tears are falling into my hands. Rhodes hugs me automatically and I can't help but let him. I shake in his arms, and the images overwhelm me.

In my mind it's Sunday again, and I'm back in Johannesburg.

*

We spoke little over breakfast that morning. Yusuf had left and the dining table was already associated with things unsaid.

I knew Rhodes would drink at the conference, but I was surprised to see him bring the quarter-bottle of whiskey he'd brought back from the city the night before. I told him it wouldn't help but he wandered off and started speaking loudly to people in Afrikaans. I mingled, spoke with Yusuf, lost sight of Rhodes.

I didn't see him until we broke for lunch. Everyone convened in the main hall for buffet food. I guessed correctly that he'd skipped the morning's talks, and that he'd already finished the whiskey. But something trivial had put him in a good mood – perhaps he'd met a like-minded Afrikaner. I knew it was only the volatile good humour of a drunk.

I tried to relax him but couldn't. He started bothering the Americans who he'd shown his Harley to the morning before. They edged away. Then he made a public display of opening a beer bottle with his teeth, something I hadn't seen him do since before New Promise. I tugged his arm and told him to simmer down. He started singing. When I told him again, he turned.

'I'm an adult.'

'Act like one.' I should've dropped it. 'You're embarrassing me.'

I whispered that I knew he was upset about last night, but that we'd have plenty of time to talk everything over when we got home.

'Nothing to say. You're not taking my son out of school.'

'Our son. Besides, it'll be a joint decision.'

'Exactly. And I'm saying no.'

I tried to draw him away from the centre of the room but he wouldn't budge. People were looking.

'He's not going.'

'Rhodes.'

'No.' He tottered. 'He's not going.'

The beer-bottle fell out of his hand and bounced awkwardly on the carpet. I picked it up and kept it. An empty circle formed around us.

'Rhodes, you're drunk. I'm leaving.'

I was about to go when it happened. It was so sudden and messy and public.

Rhodes opened his mouth and the words fell out of him greasy and devastating. 'I'm not letting my boy grow up like a barefoot *kaffir*.'

And that was it. The word, carrying with it all the pain and hatred of the past, tumbled clumsily into a weekend full of talk of the future. The delegates around us fell silent as their pity descended upon me. Their hatred and fear of Rhodes settled in the air around us. 'Poor woman,' they must have been thinking, 'The only person of colour at the entire conference and her husband shouts the word "*kaffir*" at her.' Already the Americans had guessed by the crowd's reaction what it meant. The shame was complete.

I looked around for Yusuf. He didn't come forward.

I ran out of the conference hall in a blur and met the streets of Johannesburg blinded by tears. I slumped down there, anonymous, and all the passing people of the Black capital saw a sight so commonplace they might barely have noticed. A woman of colour, crying on the pavement.

*

The train is pulling into Cape Town. We sit opposite each other, Rhodes and I, watching the townships take shape. My mother grew up in a place like that, after her family was displaced from the city, before she met my father. They raised me to value the same freedom and contentment they wished for everyone. They would understand little, I think, of the relative discomfort of New Promise Farm, but they might have understood my desire to create a better world for my family.

Now we're returning to that better world, but my images of it are cold and overcast. I see the broken pump of the borehole, the cracks in the ferrocement. I see the Port Jackson willow, impossible to clear, choking the native fynbos and our vegetables and livelihood, surrounding the main house, bearing down on us.

I have no idea what will happen tonight, when Rhodes's parents have gone, and Dion is in bed. I have no idea what Rhodes and I will say to each other, if anything. I don't know what will happen to the farm or to my family. For this moment, like my mother boarding the bus to take her out of town, the certainty of the absolute present is the only certainty there is.

So we alight at Cape Town in the chaos of baggage and the crowd.

Brave

Georgia Cowley

Georgia Cowley is currently studying Children's Literature and Illustration at Goldsmith's. She previously studied Psychology and Child Development, and much of her writing is inspired by her experiences supporting children with learning and mental health difficulties. She aspires to write and illustrate picture-books for children, with a focus on providing positive messages surrounding mental wellbeing. This poem was inspired by the heart-breaking death of Caroline Flack last year.

Once there was a little girl,
Who'd never whinge or pine.
She always had smile for you,
Her name was Caroline.

When all the other little girls,
Blubbed and brayed and bawled,
They said, 'Why can't you be like her?'
Then turn away, appalled.

And when she fell and scraped her knee
They'd rush on her with praise:
'Our Caroline would never cry.'
'Our Caroline's so brave.'

Until one day small, wirey threads,
Of sadness, hurt and doubt,
Sprouted deep in Caroline,
And found no pathway out.

They tangled up inside of her,
They'd twist her, pinch and pull.
They grew and grew all over her,
Till Caroline was full.

Soon the tangled spider's web,
Formed a knotty noose,
And Caroline began to fear,
She'd never pry them loose.

Still our girl did not cry out,
Even as she died,
Keeping in the messy thoughts
We've all been taught to hide.

'How terrible' They all bemoaned
standing at her grave.
'If only she had asked our help.'
'If she only she'd been brave.'

An Maighdeann-Roin

James Skivington

James Skivington has published four books, two fiction and two non-fiction. For the last few years, he has concentrated on writing stage plays and has had four performed, with another two waiting in the wings. He has just finished writing his first radio drama.

It was the odour that first alerted him. Of course, they had often smelled something similar in the few weeks since they had moved into Rockport Lodge on the Northeast coast of County Antrim. The salt on the sea breeze, the tang of seaweed and the driftwood cast onto the beach, odours that seemed to bring an added vibrancy into their new life, almost a promise of adventure. Yet there was something else about this odour, something vaguely familiar, though he could not think what it might be.

His wife had insisted that they get a house beside the sea, that she felt so much better within sight and smell of it. But as the man sat there in the semi-darkness of the big living-room, his wife away on a visit and his ten-year-old daughter asleep upstairs, he sniffed the air again and knew that this time it was different. There was a sweetness there and a kind of muskiness too that made him wonder if a fox had passed close to the house, though he knew that all the windows and doors should be closed against the cold of the night. And still that nagging feeling that he had encountered this odour somewhere before. Slowly he looked around the room and out through the windows but saw nothing untoward.

They had fallen into the habit of leaving the curtains open at night so that they could admire the view, the beach and the sea, not fifty yards away, the dark bulk of the headlands, the lights of the village across the bay. At the far window, their Christmas tree lights twinkled up at the stars, which blinked in reply. Now and then the moon, emerging from behind a cloud, threw a pale-yellow beam across the dark, placid water. The plashing of the waves on sand was so gentle that he could barely hear it.

And then, seemingly of its own accord, a door slowly opened, wider and wider, until it almost touched the wall. He sat forward in his chair, eyes wide, heart suddenly

95

pounding. He strained his eyes to look into the darkened kitchen. Nothing. He looked around him, at the windows, at the fireplace, behind him at another door and, seeing nothing out of its appointed place, began to feel a little foolish. Yet when he turned back to look at the open door to the kitchen, there she was. He tried to stifle a sudden gasp, but it escaped him and seemed to reverberate through the silence. At first, he thought it was his daughter, come down from her bedroom to get a glass of water, for the girl was about the same age, but his daughter's hair had never been in ringlets to the shoulders, *she* had never worn a string of shells around her neck nor a long white dress above black buttoned boots. And oh, that face, with its skin so white and those large, almost liquid eyes. The voice, when it came, was strangely low, almost husky.

'Do you know, sir, where my mother is?'

The man was incapable of replying and simply stared at the girl. She walked slowly across the room and looked down at his daughter's presents beneath the Christmas tree, stooped and ran her fingers over one of them. She let out a low sound, almost a growl, then turned to him.

'Has she come for me, sir?'

'I - I don't know your mother,' he managed to say, though his throat was tightening as he spoke. 'What's your name?'

'Ursilla,' she told him.

This was as a hammer blow to his chest, for that was his daughter's name, insisted upon by her mother. As the man clutched the arms of his chair and was enveloped in a fog of fear and incomprehension, the girl walked across the room and into the kitchen. After a moment's hesitation, the man leapt from his chair, ran out of the room and into the hallway. He bounded up the stairs two at a time and ran to his daughter's bedroom. His heart thumping, his breath coming in short bursts, his trembling hand turned the handle and slowly opened the door. He strained to see in the darkness, but as his eyes became accustomed to the low light, he saw that his daughter was sleeping peacefully in her bed.

Back in the living-room he looked around. The girl was gone. He felt a cold draught and going towards the kitchen he heard a sound like the bark of a dog, once, clear and sharp, then once again. In the kitchen the French windows were open, the sea beyond flat and calm and dark, with the moon emerging from behind the clouds. That is when he saw it in the water, the dark head glittering with wetness in the pale light. It was a large dog seal, looking towards the beach and it gave another single, loud bark. At once a higher-pitched, answering bark came from a cluster of rocks. That is when the man saw her, the strange girl, walking down onto the sand, her long ringlets, her white dress ruffled by the breeze. As she went, she appeared to be draping some kind of hooded cloak over her shoulders. She stepped into the water. The man wanted to shout, 'No, no, what are you doing?' And yet so mesmerised was he by the scene that he could say and do nothing, but merely stood with his hands tightly clutching the door frame.

Slowly the girl waded into the sea, the dark cloak billowing behind her on the water until she pulled it tightly around her body and lifted the top over her head, which was all that was now showing as she swam out to the dog seal. He growled a greeting and this was answered by the girl. Then the two of them swam away from the beach and just before the moon went behind a cloud, the man seemed to see the heads of two seals, before they were gone into the depths below and he was left wondering if there had been anything there at all.

When his wife returned home two days later, he was so much in doubt about the reality of his experience that he told her what *appeared* to have happened. She was dismissive, saying that he must have fallen asleep and dreamt the whole thing. Over the next few days, he almost came to believe this himself and wondered why he had even mentioned the incident, which, at this remove, seemed more incredible than ever. However, on Christmas morning, as his daughter played with her presents from beneath the tree, the man saw that she was wearing a shell necklace, very similar to that worn by the strange girl. When he asked her where she got it, his daughter said that she had found it, wrapped in seaweed, amongst her presents. Her mother said that it had probably been dropped by one of her daughter's friends, but neither mother nor daughter seemed to make any effort to find out who that might have been. The man said nothing, though each time he thought about the incident, he had a hollow feeling in the pit of his stomach and the return of the faint memory that he had smelled that unusual odour somewhere else.

It was some months later when the man heard the tale of the newborn baby girl, wrapped in seaweed and wearing only a string of shells around her neck, being found outside the kitchen door of Rockport Lodge many years before. At the time, the locals had said that the child must have been left there by an *maighdeann-roin*, a seal-woman. It was certainly an interesting story but surely just another fairy tale, along with those about leprechauns and haunted houses, which had once been common in the Glens. The man smiled at his own naivety and told no-one else about his experience.

One day, in search of an old book, he went into one of the storerooms at the side of the house. Looking out of the window and across the sea, towards Garron Point in the distance, he suddenly smelled the strange, musky odour once again, stronger this time. Catching his breath, he turned quickly, his eyes raking over the boxes, the bags, the old furniture that almost filled the room. Then slowly he moved amongst them, head bent, sniffing here and there. Nothing. Until he came to the old cabin trunk.

It belonged to his wife, who had said that it contained mementoes of times past, of her first husband, of a lost child. He knelt on the floor beside it. Now the smell was even stronger. When he tried to lift the lid, he found that it was locked. He stared at it for a few moments and then decided. He had to find out what was in there. He jumped up and left the room, shortly returning with a screwdriver. The hasp on the lock came away quite easily and yet he paused before slowly opening the lid and being assaulted by the very strong odour. He grimaced and peered inside.

At first it was hard to distinguish what was in the trunk, but as he opened the lid wider, he could see that it was some kind of skin, dark grey mottled with a lighter tone, dry and bristly. He pulled at the topmost part and it lifted in one piece. There was no doubt about it. It was a small sealskin and underneath it was a larger one. There was nothing else in the trunk. Slowly he closed the lid and gazed out through the window.

When he told his wife what he had found, she was very angry, saying that he had no right to break open the trunk, that these things were her personal possessions. She refused to discuss the relevance of the sealskins and said that the matter was now closed. But in truth that was far from the case, for, somewhere in the middle of that night, he awoke to find his wife gone from their bed and heard the sighing of wind as through a half-open door. He arose and looked out of the window. A lemon moon was shimmering across the waters of the bay. Then, at the edge of the rocks in front of the house, he saw two figures hurrying towards the sea. One was his wife, holding a bundle of material and behind her she pulled their daughter Ursilla.

In one horrifying instant all was clear to the man, the strange girl, the necklace, the sealskins and the tale of *an maighdeann-roin*. He raced out of the room and almost flung himself down the stairs. Anything but his beloved Ursilla! Through the kitchen and out of the open back door he went, bounding across the path, the sharp stones stabbing blood from his bare feet. Now the two figures were at the edge of the water. His wife had pulled on what he now realised was the larger of the two sealskins and was wrapping the smaller one around Ursilla.

'No!' he screamed. 'No, you can't do this! Ursilla, come back!'

Eyes wide, she turned to look at him. Her mother dragged her towards the lapping waves.

They entered the water as the man ran out onto the sand. It was then that he saw, a little further out, the head of a dog seal and another, smaller one nearby. The dog seal gave a sharp bark. Now mother and daughter were waist deep in the sea. The man sprinted across the sand and threw himself into the water after them. He swam as hard and as fast as he had ever done in his life. As he got to them, the water was up to their shoulders.

'Ursilla, no, no!' he screamed and reached out for her. The girl, staring-eyed, confused, turned to look at him. Her mother tried to pull her away. The dog seal barked. Then the man managed to grasp the shell necklace around his daughter's neck. He wrenched at it and as it broke and sank down through the dark water it was as though a key had been turned. Ursilla immediately pulled herself away from her mother's grasp and clung to her father. The woman, the mother, *an maighdeann-roin*, without a glance backwards, swam out to the other two seals. There were barked greetings before three seals slipped beneath the water.

On the beach, the man and his daughter stood clinging to each other, shivering and crying, their tears mingling with the beads of sea water on their cheeks, their faces glistening in the wan light of the moon. It was not many weeks before they left Rockport Lodge and found themselves a new home, many miles inland, far from the sea and those who live in it.

He Carries Me

Georgia Jones

Georgia is a Senior Lecturer at Bournemouth University, where she specialises in predator ecology and conservation; she currently works on sharks, birds of prey and mustelids. Georgia has acquired quite the menagerie, including two dogs, a cat, two parrots, three chickens and a pony! Her husband knew what he was letting himself in for when he married her. She loves to surf, rock climb, ride horses, skateboard and she writes when the feeling takes her.

Peering across the void
Sensing stardust and heartbeat
Seeing into muscle, blood and bone
He carries me

Centring in sunshine
Taking up space in the rain
Finding give and resolution
He carries me

My best self and my worst
Seeking congruence always
Practicing integrity and truth
He carries me

Terrain and tasks ephemeral
Rhythm constant and timeless
Feeling tribal, raw and right
He carries me

Lost

Jen Hall

Jen Hall is a fundraiser from the South West of England. She writes about the power of female friendships, and the undercurrent of violence in our society.

'Excuse me, you dropped something.' I call at a man.

It doesn't look important, this thing. It fell out his back pocket; it could be a receipt. But it might be a train ticket. Or a locker receipt – you can leave bags and coats on hangers in museums nowadays.

He doesn't turn around at the sound of my voice, but it's a busy street. How would he know it's him I'm talking to? I walk over and pick it up. It is a train ticket. For a morning train, with a stamp on it to say it's been used. The stamp is a raised impression and in slightly green ink. It's probably rubbish. He may not notice he's lost it. Or he might need it. People need receipts for expenses; you have to prove that you bought things to prove you're not stealing. I get my trolley and follow after him.

He's walking briskly; he has somewhere to go. It's a struggle to keep up. I'm slower than him as I have all my things. The bottom of my trolley sags and drags along the pavement sometimes, and the wheels splay out. But it's still useful. Easier than carrying all my bags. The bags are important to keep things organised.

Finally, the man turns into a quieter road, and I'm relieved I've caught up with him. He hears me this time when I shout: 'Excuse me sir, you dropped this.'

He looks at me, and barely glances at the ticket I'm holding out towards him.

'It's not mine.' he says. He has that dismissive voice, and a frown on his face. As if I can't possibly have anything of his. It reminds me of my husband when I told him I was pregnant.

It's not mine.

'It is. I saw you drop it.' *It is, it can't be anyone else's.*

'It doesn't matter anyway.' *You can't prove it's mine.* He walks away. I tuck the ticket into a bag in my trolley. I have a bag for paperwork. Receipts, bills, letters. A lot of train tickets. It's important to keep hold of things. You never know when you might start to miss them. If I have things organised, I might be able to help when someone realises what they've lost. I turn my trolley and walk back the way I came, back towards my part of town.

It's a loud night tonight. It must be a weekend. Boys shouting. Girls shrieking – in fun most of the time. I don't think I hear any pain. It's dark, but the heat of the day is still here. The air smells of warm tarmac. The ground is dry. People lose different things at this time of year. They don't have all the extras needed for winter – no gloves or scarves or extra coats. In this weather, people lose sunglasses. Or beads dropping from broken necklaces. Sometimes girls lose shoes in this weather. High-heeled, strappy ones. They can walk barefoot on the streets when they're dry and warm. It's dangerous – you might step in dog mess, cigarette butts or glass. But falling off those shoes looks dangerous too. I feel proud of these girls with the confidence to walk and throw caution to the wind. They hardly even need their shoes.

I bring you everything you need. The words drummed into my head are still there now.

I keep hold of their shoes. Just in case. Maybe in the daylight their confidence would drop away, and they'd need their shoes.

A boy drops some food. I don't like talking to boys; it can be dangerous. But he might be hungry later. I hesitate for a moment while I decide, then the words burst out of me.

'You dropped something!' I shout at him. He hears me and looks towards me. I point at his food, and he replies to me.

'Why don't you pick it up then? Lazy cow!' His friends laugh.

I blink at his words, and the echo they create from

another time. *It's a tip in here. What do you do all day? Lazy cow.*

It's safer not to argue. I drop my pointed finger, and curl my arm back in. The boy is walking towards me.

'I said you should pick it up,' he says, standing in front of me. I don't want to leave my things. I'm worried about my things. But it's easier to do what they ask. Less chance of violence. Perhaps.

Do some fucking cleaning for once.

I walk over to his food and pick it up.

'Now put it in the bin. You don't deserve my leftovers.'

You don't deserve to eat. I have to work. You can have some food when you've worked for it.

I close the polystyrene lid and drop it carefully into the bin. He walks away. I could feel that it was still hot. I wait until he's definitely gone before I collect it from the bin.

A woman drops a pound coin at my feet.

'You dropped this!' I say and hold it out to her. I start to get up, to follow her and return it.

'It's for you, don't get up.' My legs start to ache as I crouch between sitting and standing. I'm not sure what to do now.

You sit on your arse all day. Get out of my way you stupid bitch. There's never a right answer.

'Do you need a hot drink?' she asks. I shake my head. Hot drinks can be dangerous.

Stupid Cow! You've burnt my tongue. A long-gone scream rattles around my head as too-hot coffee is poured over my baby. *See – you'd have made me drink something that hot?* Best to stay away from hot drinks.

'Anything to eat? I could get you a sandwich?' The woman is still there, looking at me. I can feel tears boiling up in my head. I didn't think I could cry any more.

A different voice repeats in my head this time. A

neighbour, shouting through my letter box. *You're worse than an animal. Letting him starve like that.*

This woman in front of me is talking to me like I'm a person. I carry on getting up, gathering my things. Time to move on. She's seen me, but I can't let her see the real me. I feel her disappointment in me as I move down the street.

I'm trying to read my book in the park. My eyes are still good, but the light is too bright. The book was lost. I found it near a bench, but I didn't see anyone drop it. I sat on the bench and held it for a while in case someone came back. Sometimes people don't realise when they've lost something.

I waited with the book for a whole day. I hear a policeman's voice, an echo of disgust from years ago. *You just sat there and waited while he died.*

Lots of people walk one way to work, and then the same way back again. Someone might have come past looking for it. I put it on the bench beside me. I don't mean to, but I think I make things invisible.

Why didn't you try and get help?

People try so hard not to see me, that they don't see the things around me either.

I sit quietly, and hope I'm doing the right thing. If I'm just waiting, nothing bad that happens is my fault.

Why didn't you try and get help?

I tried to help that person who lost their book. The book is mine now. I waited long enough.

A baby drops a sock off the end of its toes. That happens a lot. Baby socks are one of the things I have most of. That and gloves. Odd gloves, one at a time. Rarely a pair. Enough for a bag full. Sometimes I give the gloves to my friends when it is really cold. The ones I've had the longest, that people are definitely not coming back for.

'Your baby dropped a sock,' I call, and the woman looks

back. She sees it lying, lost on the pavement.

'Thank you,' she says to me. She puts the sock back on to her kicking baby. Mumbling about what a pickle he is. She saw me. She heard me. Voices from people I've never even met jumble in my head. Voices on television, people in the supermarket, jumping out from the newspaper.

Didn't anyone hear the baby crying?

The sock wasn't lost.

Social Services should have been checking on them.

If people notice me, I can make sure things aren't lost.

A Poem In Which I'm No Longer Afraid

Ana Reisens

Ana Reisens is an emerging poet and writer with a background in translation. She was recently awarded the Barbara Mandigo Kelly Peace Poetry Award and you can find her poetry forthcoming in Inkwell Journal and Subterranean Blue. She's working on her first poetry collection and a novel, and can be reached at anareisens@gmail.com.

& suddenly I'm running.
The air is thick & my limbs

are weak but I've seized my heels
& I'm out the door & onto the street.

The night is old & I've forgotten my coat
but I've found my skin & I'm no longer cold

& the city is throwing its nets of smoke
but I've taken back my nostrils, my lungs

& my throat. My legs are lightening
as the sky is brightening & the grey

is tightening its aching hold, as the pavement
shakes under the weight of my bones.

Now a crowd has gathered to stand in my way
but they can't dam the rivers of my veins

because I've seized my elbows, my liver, my fists,
as the men in blue reach for my wrists

& the women cry out, they need my hips,
but I've taken them back, all of it, it's mine –

my shoulders & ovaries & hamstrings
& bile – & the fingers of the past are tugging

at my form but not even memory
can contain me anymore.

I reach the edge as my vision clears
& suddenly my mother appears.

She's holding a spark like a firefly in a jar
& it's all that's left & I've come so far

so I pry open her hands
as my story lifts away –

Thank you, I say,
but I'll be taking it from here.

Thirty-Six Up

Bethany Wren

Bethany graduated from Royal Holloway, University of London's Creative Writing MA with a distinction in 2020. She is currently working on a novel, while finishing off the short story collection started in her Master's, and writing ad hoc short stories. She was highly commended for her following story by industry judges, Anna Khan Khattak and Sophie Scard. She was longlisted for the London Library Emerging Writers Programme in 2020.

Malcolm can't see who's out there on the Beinn.

The mist will disappear soon, he knows that. It creeps over the mountain every morning, like a bad omen, lifting by the time he has finished his first cup of tea. Sometimes it will come back during the day, dropping from the clouds so thick and fast that Malcolm will grumble because even his state-of-the-art telescope can't penetrate that kind of fog.

On this particular morning, everything is soft and blurry; the sun obscured, the mountainside a mystery. He can't see it, but Malcolm likes knowing that underneath it all, it is the same as it ever was.

There is a barometer hanging on the wall. Its needle has swung to *Fair* overnight.

'A good day for climbing,' he says, quietly.

He settles into his seat, putting his hands around the telescope, enjoying its cool edges beneath his fingers. It takes him a moment to find the right spot on the path, but here it is. He blinks a few times, adjusting to the sensation of closing one eye while the other strains into the eyepiece.

Around him, the spare bedroom is a mess. Maps and charts line the surfaces; books are piled up on the bed. On the wall hangs a painting of the mountain by a local artist, all soft blues and greens. Fluffy white clouds. It's such a simplified version of what Malcolm looks at every day in sharp, unrelenting detail, it makes him smile every time he notices it.

Despite the mess, there's something peaceful about this spot in the spare room. The chair is pulled up to the window. His fingers are poised over his instrument, the only place they do not tremble. His back aches as he leans forward. Not long until the first ones will arrive.

The notebook in his lap is running out of pages. *Tuesday 3rd April*, he writes at the top of the page in his best handwriting, the 'y' looping further than he had intended, the ends of the letters running away from him. He underlines the heading with two straightish lines.

With his eye fixed back in place on the telescope, he realigns his view and waits. As predicted, the mist is already diminishing, the glory of Ben Nevis revealing herself. The radiator clicks beneath the window. Downstairs, his wife moves around. Malcolm doesn't mean to, but he holds his breath.

Finally, he sees them: two figures walking up the path. Men. They are chatting animatedly, one gesticulating as the other laughs. Malcolm focuses in on their lips, trying to understand what they're saying, but they're moving too fast and he can't keep the telescope focused on their faces for long enough. Within a minute, they have scaled to the top of the path and are turning round the corner, past Malcolm's vision and onto the next section of the track.

07.36 am. Two men. Red coat and beard / green hat, he writes.

This particular part of the path is about half an hour from the base of the mountain. It's rocky, usually frosty on mornings like this, the particles of ice clinging to the rock in patches – odd and uneven. It'll be much worse when they turn the corner, and the higher they get, the whiter it will become, until there's thick snow for the last hour or so.

Malcolm has seen a lot of unprepared tourists in his time, those walking up the path in sandals – or worse, flip flops. He has considered adding another column to his table for his own amusement: *footwear*. But sometimes he barely has time to write down the time and description, let alone what kind of shoes they are wearing. This is an important job, and he shouldn't make light of it.

Malcolm is no artist; he is a record keeper.

He hums under his breath as he watches the men disappear from view. It's always exciting to see the first ascenders of the day. There's something hopeful about it; he gets to witness the beginning of their journey. He has no control over the rest of the path, but here he can see. He can write what he sees.

He can do something useful.

Next comes a middle-aged man and woman, both red-faced and panting.

08.02 am. Couple. Unfit.

Not far behind them, another couple. These two are younger, blonde-haired and tanned.

08.15 am. Couple. Fast, probably Scandinavian.

There's two women, a man, a woman, and then a larger group. They are led by a woman with an unusually big forehead and a pink scarf. She is talking, her mouth moving quickly.

08.18 am. Two women. Silly hats.

08.29 am. Lone man. Dark hair, foreign.

08.46 am. Lone woman. Young, yellow coat.

08.55 am. Group. Seven persons (three men and four women), another rambling group led by an aspiring dictator.

There's a rumbling noise from over the road that distracts him for a moment. Malcolm removes his eye from the telescope and watches as Pat from number 52 takes in the bins. The woman next door is buckling her screaming child into the backseat of her car. He holds onto the telescope, not wanting to let it go. It's the opportunity to see more than this.

A gift from his son, at first Malcolm didn't know what to make of the telescope. Bresser Venus AZ. It came in a box with so many letters and numbers on it, Malcolm was sure he wouldn't even understand how to build it.

They had assembled it together, his son tightening the screws, taking the parts from Malcolm's unsteady hands.

'She's watched over you your whole life,' his son said, pointing up at Ben Nevis, looming and magnificent. 'Now it's your turn to watch over her. You'll get a perfect view from up here. It'll be something to do while you get better.'

It had been almost frightening to look through the eyepiece for the first time, to see life magnified in this way. He felt like some omniscient god, peering down onto the world, watching its inhabitants go about their daily life. And then he had moved his gaze up onto the mountain path, watched people go up and go down, and everything had changed.

At night he dreams of counting people, of seeing them pass in front of him in a straight line, writing them down in his notebook. They always come back down; he makes sure of it.

At 12.30, his wife brings him a tuna sandwich, his tablets perched alongside the bread.

'How many are you up to?' she asks, placing the plate on his desk.

'Thirty-six up,' he says. 'They'll be starting to come down soon.'

'Mmm,' she says, tiding some papers and plumping his cushion. 'Shall we have a glass of wine tonight? We could sit in the conservatory. It's getting lovely and light in the evenings.'

'When they're all down, maybe.'

'Ok,' she says, and he hears her making her way downstairs and into the kitchen, singing along to a song on the radio.

'Turn that down,' he calls. 'I can't concentrate.'

After a moment, there's silence again.

He glances at his notebook. At 07.36 am, the first two men ascended. They looked in good condition, had walking sticks and suitable footwear, not too overweight, going at a good pace. By his estimations, they should be coming down at any moment, assuming they stayed at the top for the average amount of time.

He puts his eye to the telescope and, there they are – red coat male and green hat traipsing down, looking in good spirits and still going at a good pace. He ticks their names off, writing *12.38* in the final column.

Two down, 34 to go.

One by one, the walkers come back down the mountain, and Malcolm is disappointed to see that they descend in the same order they went up. It's a boring day on Ben Nevis when nobody has overtaken anybody else. The red-faced couple comes down the track. There's the Scandinavian pair, the man with dark hair, the walking group with the bossy woman looking slightly dishevelled now.

At 16.45, he begins adding up each person's individual climb time. His wife is downstairs hoovering. The sound of the vacuum grates against him, just like the radio, the kettle, the slamming of a door – anything that is not complete silence. He tuts to himself as he fills in the final column, trying to drown out the roar of the hoover with his own sound. She is always doing something to irritate him nowadays.

Then he notices something.

It can't be.

The breath falls out of him as he looks at his chart again.

A return time is missing.

He stares at his notebook for a long time, frowning and trying to think. *Lone woman. Young, yellow coat.* She was after the foreign man and before the walking group, but clearly, she hasn't come down yet, otherwise there would be a time written in the space, which is blank and looking up at him now, incandescent with its emptiness.

Heart racing, he puts an eye back to the telescope and

looks at the path again. For several minutes he watches the empty path, waiting for the woman in the yellow coat to come back down. Maybe it took her longer to get up there. Maybe she got tired and is walking slowly. Maybe she stopped for a while at the top – chatting with the others, taking photos, writing a poem.

But she wouldn't stay long. The snow up there will be deep at this time of year, the wind biting.

So maybe –

But he doesn't want to think about that. He waits, squinting so hard his other eye hurts, holding his breath until the moment he sees her rounding the corner. She has to come down again.

An hour passes and Malcolm doesn't move, but there is no sign of the woman in the yellow coat.

He taps his fingers now against his lap and thinks what he should do. Images flash though his mind – the woman on the ground, clutching at her ankle. Her cries for help echoing around the mountainside that will soon begin to get dark. It's harsh up there, Malcolm knows that. There have been accidents and deaths on the mountain his whole life. He's grown up in the shadow of Ben Nevis, and the danger she holds.

That's why he's never been up there himself.

Another ten minutes pass and finally Malcolm stands, as fast as he can manage, and creaks over to the doorway, through the hallway and down the stairs. He's at the front door, lacing up his boots with shaking fingers when his wife asks, 'What are you doing, dear?'

'There's a woman,' he says, fetching his scarf and hat from the cupboard. 'She didn't come down. Thirty-six up and thirty-five down.'

He tries to open the front door, but the keys are in the lock and he can't turn them hard enough. Everything has been much more difficult since the diagnosis, and now he can't even open the bloody front door to his own house.

His wife looks at him in amazement.

'You can't be serious. You're not well enough to go out.'

But Malcolm's not listening. He's fumbling with the key, willing his fingers to grip it hard enough to turn.

'How are you going to get there?' she asks.

'You can drive me,' says Malcolm, finally able to turn the keys and open the front door with a sigh of relief. 'Come on.'

Whether in acquiescence or shock, his wife grabs her coat and car keys and helps him into the car. She talks the whole way, muttering under her breath.

'Doesn't leave the house for a year,' he hears her say. 'And now this.'

Every now and again, she turns to look at him with wide eyes, as if she can't quite recognise the man sitting in the passenger seat.

They reach the car park at the visitor centre and Malcolm makes his way shakily out of the car, walking towards the bridge over the river where the path starts.

'Malcolm!' shouts his wife, trying to stop him, but for the first time in many months, Malcolm is walking unaided, shuffling as fast as he can. He thinks of the woman in the yellow coat and how frightened she must be, up there alone. It's getting cold now.

If he can make it to her in time, he can save her.

He hears his name being called as he presses forward, trying not to trip over the loose stones on the ground. He didn't bring his walking stick and didn't think of it until now, but suddenly he feels its absence keenly. He is unbalanced and wobbly. Every step is difficult, but somehow, he is managing.

He looks ahead every few moments, desperately seeking

any sign of a yellow coat. But the mountainside is muted, grey and green. The light has changed now. Great clouds are rolling in and it can mean only one thing – there will be fresh snow tonight. He already knows what the barometer in the spare room will say. *Stormy.*

Malcolm can't hear the shouting behind him anymore. Here, at last, is his silence, breath-taking in its magnitude. It is empty and wonderful and frightening as he stops to breathe it in.

What a thing it is to be here at last.

But now there's a noise behind him. Puffing, as his wife finally reaches him and grabs his shoulder with her cold fingers.

'Malcolm!' she screams at him, although he is right in front of her and can hear her perfectly well.

'I need to –' he says without looking at her, but she interrupts him breathlessly.

'The woman came back down hours ago. I asked at the visitor centre.'

Malcolm stops, but he doesn't turn towards his wife. Instead, he looks up at the mountain ahead of him, at the winding track that disappears and reappears on the other side of a gorge. There are other peaks up ahead, snow-covered and defiant.

The woman is alive and well. All that worrying had been for nothing. All that counting and recounting had been wrong. He is relieved, of course.

But, as he looks up at the path, his heart pulls a little. He feels a loss of something, of what he is not quite sure.

He turns to face his wife and sees her rosy-cheeked and wild-haired before him, her eyes filled with worry. She reaches out her hand to him and he takes one last look up at the path before they make their way back down the yellow-less Ben Nevis and towards the car.

Keeper Of Walks

Gail Mosley

Let's just say I'll miss the long-legged stride,
single file or alongside,
me on the right for the good ear,
walking, talking, listening,
or, like as not, easy with quiet.

Stopping to breathe.
Noticing treecreeper, robin, red kite,
a familiar flower, name, forgotten, found
in the rain-speckled wildflower book.

Searching out lunchtime perches,
riverbanks, tree stumps, walls, boulders,
bird hides,
sheltered churchyard benches.

Puzzling over maps
for the path, barn, field corner,
ready to retrace steps,
down here, yes, back on track.
Owning every walk.

I am the keeper now.

Starting Again

Sandra Srivastava

Sandra has had several travel articles published and has completed a travel book. She began writing fiction in 2020 as she was unable to travel and take photos to accompany her non-fiction work. She has had several short stories published and accepted for publication, and is working on a novel. She is a former lawyer and holds a Master's degree in Cornish Studies. Her email address is srivvy@yahoo.com.

I park my car – my pride and joy, an elegant red Volvo - at the roadside, facing my old college. I have not seen the college since I was a student here in the 1970s. I have made a few brief visits to the town to see family and friends, who have now all moved away, and I have had no reason to come. But just recently, I have felt a strange urge to see the college and my old home. After leaving here, I will drive to the other side of the town to see my old home, stay in a B&B nearby, and then tour the town by car before going home; I never actually liked the town, yet now it seems newly important.

When I look at a place I have not seen for a long time, naturally I imagine it as it was then, not as it is now. If I were to go inside, it would look as it did then, the same people would be there, they would be dressed the same, they would talk about the same things, they would carry the same bags and books. I am not sure I want to go in.

I walk slowly towards the entrance. What if I am challenged, and have to explain myself? What if I am saddened by the changes that will undoubtedly have taken place? But I am compelled to go in, whatever the consequences.

My ankles feel wet. I look down and see that the backs of my trousers – wide flares, just like those I used to wear, and which I always ensured were wider than anyone else's - are touching the ground and are ragged where they have been dragged along the pavement. Water has leached up the bottom few inches – *inches*, not centimetres.

My back is no longer aching from the weight of my trusty rucksack, containing large wallet, smartphone and various gadgets that I carry everywhere. Instead, I'm carrying an even heavier briefcase, stuffed with large books. I haven't had one of these since ... I left college.

I push open the door. I need to get rid of some of the

weight. Somehow, I realise that if I have a locker, and its key, I will be just another student, and no-one will notice me. In my briefcase, instead of the wallet full of plastic cards and paper money, is a little purse, containing only a few coins for emergency phone calls, a front-door key and a locker key. I don't know why I expected anything else.

I climb the stairs, turn left, and there are the lockers, outside my old tutor room. I think I remember which is mine. I turn the key and – hey presto – the door opens. From the briefcase I take out my empty, old-fashioned lunchbox. I don't remember eating the former contents, but at least I know it's the afternoon and I was here this morning. I find a dog-eared timetable tucked in the back of a notebook. 'What day is it?' I ask.

'Tuesday,' says a familiar voice.

I turn around. There, in front of me, is Claire, my best friend in college days. We kept in touch for some years, then gradually saw less of each other when we had moved to different parts of the country. What I really want to say is, 'Wow! How are you? You've hardly changed in decades!' But, since I probably saw her this morning, I say, 'Oh, hi. It's geography now. Are you coming?'

I leave the lunchbox and most of the textbooks in my locker, and let Claire lead the way to the geography room.

After geography I go to the common room, just to see who's around. As I open the door, the sound of a jingly 1970s tune comes blasting out at me. Brilliant! I go in, and there are plenty of familiar faces; somehow it seems perfectly normal to see them there.

At the end of the college day, people start drifting off home. I go out of the gates, and stop briefly – how am I going to get home? Do I have a driving lesson today? No, in the place where my instructor usually parks is an elegant, red Volvo. I admire it as I walk past on my way to the bus stop. I take out a tattered bus pass made of yellow card, flash it at the driver, go upstairs to my favourite seat at the front, and spend a pleasant twenty minutes gazing out of the windows at places that haven't changed.

I get off the bus and walk towards my old home. Somehow, I know I have to pretend to be my teenage self. This accomplished, I will *become* ... myself.

I take out my front-door key from the tiny purse, unlock the door and step into the house. I hear a thump and know it is the cat, jumping down from the sitting-room windowsill, just as she used to do most days when I arrived home. She is not allowed to sit on the windowsill because she leaves long hairs on the net curtain, so she jumps down when she hears someone come in. I had forgotten that sound. It is coming back to me now, and I shudder; it feels too real.

The house is just as it was. I enter the dining room, and gasp when I see that Dad has regrown the long sideburns that he sported for a few years in the 1970s, and that his hair is no longer grey and thin, but black and curly again. He is sitting at the table, doing some very important paperwork, smoking and listening to the radio. The radio programme is all Harold Wilson this, Edward Heath that, all very boring. He grunts a sort of hello, and I respond with 'Um.' I could have asked all sorts of questions, but something tells me to stay in character; I was never much for words.

I go through into the kitchen, where I find Mum, wearing a pretty dress and an apron. I am startled as she starts prattling on about her day; she hasn't been able to speak for years, so I just listen appreciatively. She is making dinner - meat and two veg, and some sort of stodgy pudding, all of which have had the goodness boiled out of them. The room stinks, and the air is full of steam. Ugh!

We sit around the table, chewing the awful meal. My brother, now a skinny 13-year-old again, is sitting opposite. We glare at each other and say nothing. He is still wearing his muddy football kit; he is so football-obsessed that it does not occur to him that there is anything else in life, like being clean. Little does he know that, in a few years' time, he will have an accident, and everything will change; but how did I know that?

We go into the sitting room to watch our brand-new, 26-inch colour television. The Russians this, the Cold War that – only the grown-ups need to think about all that. I'm going to do my homework.

I go to my room. On my bed is a continental quilt, the latest fashion, adorned with a cover with an orange-and-white psychedelic pattern. The wallpaper and curtains are orange, white and brown. The carpet is orange. On the desk is a bright orange angle-poise lamp, a typewriter and a row of books.

I unpack my bag. I heave out the books and a handful of rubbish. But what's this? I don't recognise it. I turn it over in my hands. It is about six inches long, three inches wide, a quarter of an inch thick, mostly plastic, shiny on one side. I know this object should be so important that I take it everywhere and use it constantly. It feels familiar and comfortable in my hand; I feel its smoothness; I almost know what to do with it; slowly I reach out a finger as if to use it … I have that strange, disorientated feeling that you have when you are waking up after a long dream and are still mentally solving whatever problems existed in the dream.

I shrug. I must be tired. It's just some rubbish. As I chuck it in the bin with the sweet wrappers, it begins to fade until there is nothing left, and I forget about it.

I open my books.

The Bramblelands

Gracie Jack

Gracie Jack is the penname of Laura Potts, a writer from West Yorkshire. A recipient of the Foyle Young Poets Award, her work has been published by Aesthetica, The Moth and The Poetry Business. Laura became one of the BBC's New Voices in 2017. She received a commendation from The Poetry Society in 2018 and was shortlisted for The Edward Thomas Fellowship, The Rebecca Swift Women Poets' Prize and The Bridport Prize in 2020'.

Twenty years from where we were, I stand
by the garden gate watching the younger me
swinging free feet over the wall. Small,
and as young as the summer will always be,
with you and your dungarees, soil-stained
and torn, as you swallow the last

of the corner-shop sweets and the sun rolls back
on his thread. He licks the lawn into colour and
we laugh, talking over how the shadows will fold
into the sooner dawn and how a piece of old moon
will unwind on her spool, saying, *this is the way*
it is meant to be. This is the way we were born.

Today we have been wildlings and escaped
to some place in the forest where the trees play
the light through their leaves. Their arrows cling
to your skin until your hair is a chorus of gold,
until you look at me with those eyes which say, *will*
we come back here when we are old, oh when we are old?

With cracked hands we churn up a wheelbarrow
out of the shed and freewheel down to the stream.
I flip a pebble and watch it drown,
while you say *like this*, and cartwheel another.
It skitters and lives, gifted, as a blackbird trills above,
calling, *one day you will laugh and one day find love.*

Then the silver thread chimes from the back door -
a woman's soft voice and the scent of knives and forks.
We part through the fence, our secret handshake:
tomorrow we will meet on our wall and be young again.
Now, I watch from the gate as our voices spill
into our kitchens, and wonder whether you, like me,
will ever stand in the sad glamour of rain,
your eyes bright before the lights of childhood again.

Inu Irin Ajo (I Am On A Journey)

Tinu Ogunkanmi

Tinu Ogunkanmi comes from a big Nigerian blended family and is the fourth of six children. Tinu is currently in the last leg of her English degree at Bournemouth University. In her spare time, she loves reading romantic novels and watching Korean films and shows. She is thankful to her father, stepmother, and her birth mother for the sacrifices they've made for her, as well as for the joyful life they've given her.

Fired. They'd fired her. Melody still couldn't believe it as she stood there waiting on the platform. Her train had been delayed for the last 20 minutes. Something about an accident close by was all she could make out from the flurry of information that was passing through her head at a staggering speed. She was, strangely, neither here nor there. Like she was floating elsewhere and not at all standing on that Overground platform, supposedly on her way to Tia's engagement dinner.

She didn't know whether to laugh or cry but she knew her composure must be kept because 'one couldn't cry in a public place', that's what her sister had taught her. 'As black women,' she would start by saying, 'we have to behave in a certain way.' At this point in her spiel, Sarah would look Mel straight in the eyes so Mel knew she meant business. In return, Mel would internally roll her eyes. She had never really been fond of that ideology.

Music was playing through her earbuds, but she wasn't paying attention to it. *Focus Mel, FOCUS!* She couldn't keep her thoughts in order at all. She pleaded with herself, shutting her eyes tightly in an attempt to hold back the tears threatening to make an appearance. After a few beats, when she felt as though she'd successfully tightened the bolt on the cage that held her tears, she opened her eyes and let out what would be the first of many sighs to come.

She hated that she knew what was coming. The questions, the faces of pity, and the I-Told-You-Sos lingering like an unrelenting cold. She thought of the faux smile she'd have to plaster on her face for the whole night and visibly grimaced.

Why me? Mel asked herself. When she had dropped out of university five years ago, panic had set in like a wave, unable to settle. She hadn't known what to do next. And now here it was again – the panic – enveloping her in a stronghold, slowly increasing its pressure on her neck, her breath quickening, and her anxiety in complete disarray.

Bro, what am I gonna do now? Nah, but how am I gonna pay my BILLS? The voices swirling around in her head were getting louder and louder to the point that she hadn't heard her train finally approaching. A step too late it seemed; she'd missed her train.

'Fuck!' She groaned, instinctively bringing her arms to rest on her head. As if her day couldn't get any worse, Mel was officially late for the dinner. Tia was going to kill her. In fact, on her tombstone, it would read *Melody Ibukunoluwa Ayodele: 1994-2019. Unfortunately, but not shockingly, slain by a close friend.*

It was all jokes of course but everyone knew Tia's penchant for being on time (which didn't bode well with her already bad temper) and everyone knew that Mel was always late. Mel couldn't help it though. The African timing she'd grown accustomed to all her life meant that it was almost second nature to her, turning up late to events.

Mel revelled in the gush of warm wind brought by the appearance of another train. She stood on the train; her body pressed against the glass panel adjacent to the train doors. Just a few feet ahead of her, Mel spotted a family of three in the middle seating aisle huddled together. The mother was in the middle while her two children leaned on her from each side. They held onto her tightly as they tried to sleep through the monotonous whizzing of the train. Mel felt a sudden pang of jealousy shoot through her.

The minutes passed by quickly with Mel staring at the heart-warming scene in front of her. Before she knew it, Mel and her numb feet were climbing up the escalator and out of Canada Water. She sighed again and tried to orient herself to her new surroundings. Significant time had passed; the clouds were tinted pink as the opening act for the sunset, reflecting beautifully on the legions of stunning high-rise apartments circling the Thames.

Spotting the nearest crossing, she strolled towards it and waited there for the man to turn neon green in its black box. At this moment, she found herself again trapped by her thoughts. This time, however, she pondered on her identity and why she always felt like an unwelcome visitor in her own body. You see, this happened quite a lot when Melody was feeling down. She could confess only to herself in the unfavourable dark of the night that she simply hated herself. It didn't help that all the people around her were in such great positions in their lives – her sister Sarah was a big-time banker in Canary Wharf, Lara was getting promoted, Tia was getting married, and her dad was madly in love with his new girlfriend, Agnes. All so happy and content in their personal and professional lives. But where was Mel? They all knew who they were... But who was Melody Ayodele?

Maybe I should just turn back. It was still a half-hour walk to the venue, situated in Surrey Quays. Maybe she'd say she was physically ill or nauseous (they didn't have to know *right* away that she had been fired). As if they'd a mind of their own, Mel could feel her feet taking steps forward.

At least Mel could say the weather was lovely. There was a nice easy breeze in the air. Soft, with a comfortable level of heat – but that was because of the unrelenting rain from the past two days. She took in the myriad of lofty trees lining the path, the smell of their rough bark, and how sturdy they appeared. They were where they belonged. She admired that about trees.

Mel ambled like that for over 15minutes, admiring the trees and wallowing in her own sadness, until she came to a zebra crossing. She couldn't hear the loud beep of the sleek

SUV honking at her over the noise of her thoughts as she took those two steps forward. The vehicle collided with her body, sending her high into the air before bringing her back down violently to the hard gravel of the road.

Opening her eyes felt like a sensation Mel had never experienced before. Everything felt alien, and that filled her with complete dread and a new surge of anxiety. A swarm of people sped past her at lightning speed, pushing a table with a figure atop it through white double doors. Then came the voices and the shouting and the wailing. Mel took hesitant steps in the direction of these sounds, curious as to where they were coming from, before she was in complete view of her father, Sarah and Lara all sat down. Sarah was holding Lara, silently trying to console the hysterical cries coming from her.

Her dad, Timothy, stared in the direction of the double doors with an expression she'd only seen once before – at her mother's funeral. His face was bleak but so totally indifferent at the same time. Timothy couldn't look away, not this time.

'Daddy, what's going on? You're scaring me. ANSWER ME, PLEASE!' Mel screamed. She waved her hands to try and get their attention, but nothing worked; she couldn't believe that they couldn't see her. *That's not possible!* She thought as she turned away from them to slowly wander in the direction of those doors.

Melody regretted it almost immediately, as her eyes came to focus on the scene in front of her. There lay her almost lifeless body, eyes shut while two doctors and a number of nurses worked all over her. The gasp she let out sent her to her knees and she couldn't breathe. How was she here but also there? She closed her eyes and opened them again, repeating the process several times as if that would change what she was seeing. It didn't. *It's just not possible! Why me? It's always me!*

She didn't realize that she'd stood up and marched out of the room; her vision was blurry from the tears cascading down her face. Mel certainly didn't realize that a force, unrecognisable to her, was pulling her in the direction of a new set of doors – she was focused on the fact that she was dying, you see. The crying and the scattered voices of medical workers were all too much for her. So loud and so intense, her head throbbed trying to block them out. Something beckoned to her. She suddenly felt a flurry of warmth come over her, a thump in her heart, so heavy like rocks. Looking up at the doors stood just a few feet before her, with a bright light coming through from behind it, she felt compelled to go through them. Maybe here, she'd get the relief she so desperately wanted. *It cannot be any worse than this.*

With a flash from the blindingly white bright light, Melody found herself in a place that was definitely *not* the hospital.

'Wow!' She whispered, in utter shock at the sight she was viewing. In lieu of a blue sky was a remarkable celestial sky. It was completely ethereal, with amethysts and amaranths and azures all mingling in wonderful harmony.

As she walked the length of the long road, dusty and saffron in colour, Mel couldn't help asking, 'Am I bugging or is this Nigeria?' There was a line of lived-in huts with thatched roofs lining her pathway, but the weather was the biggest indicator. It was sweltering and biting in the way she remembered her dad had described to her.

'Why am I wearing *iro** and *buba**?' Melody asked herself, looking down at herself in bewilderment. She was no longer in her earlier ensemble of a white shirt, black trousers and heels. No, the *iro* and *buba* she wore instead were persimmon orange and paired with matching flip-flops.

Mel soon found something else to focus her attention on. She followed the aroma of spices that wafted by her nose and wandered onto a compound. Here on this compound, Melody was met with a long path. On each side of this dusty path were palm-fronted market stalls adorned with an array of food and accessories. She saw luminous figures – *ghosts* – of women, dressed in black *iro* and *buba*, sitting and loudly bantering while preparing food. Mel noticed that they all spoke her mother-tongue, Yoruba.

She smiled as she walked past them. It all seemed so familiar and homely. She loved their fondness of each other. Their attire and their gossip. For the first time in a very long time, Melody felt like a tree.

All so suddenly, the concurrent sounds of the chatter and laughter seemed to fade away. Just by blinking, Mel found herself at a park with a swing at its centre and other recreational apparatus scattered to the side. It was still the same dusty saffron-coloured roads, and still the same star-spangled sky. In front of her stood a familiar figure. Mel gasped when she registered who it was.

'*Aaro re nso mi**, my child.' The figure said and took a step forward, stretching out her hands to envelop Melody in an embrace. *I've missed you.* Melody stepped back, unwilling to feel the array of emotions bursting at the seams. It was her mother, Sade. She was clothed in a mix of black and royal blue *iro* and *buba* of the finest silk and chiffon. She was a slender woman, whose frown lines had deepened on her smooth cocoa skin over the years due to hard work as an underpaid nurse. In photos Mel had seen, Sade always looked perpetually tired, but here, as she stood tall and grand in front of Mel, she seemed brighter – even brighter than the other luminous figures she'd seen.

'What? You can't greet your own mother in death after

20whole years?' Sade spoke, with her beautiful gap-toothed smile that her father loved so much.

'You left me behind... and now you're here? Why? How?' Mel asked as she violently shook her head. The throbbing had returned in the tenth fold.

The park felt so serene at that moment. The large red swing set was still, as if frozen entirely. The ground looked a bit darker than it had moments ago but maybe it was Melody's imagination. All that could be heard was Mel's unsteady breathing.

Before speaking, Sade paused to take a deep breath. 'You know something, Ibukun?' She started by saying, 'When I first started my journey here, I begged and *begged* to go back. I needed more time with you, with your sister, with... my love. My sweet soulmate. I watched you all every day go through the hard times.' Remorse was etched clear as day on her face. 'I wanted to hold you and tell you that it was okay in those times you were alone... That you felt so alone... broke me inside all over again.' Sade took a break, tears pooling at the corner of her eyelids.

'You see Ibukun, you need to stop pushing people away and let yourself heal. You are not alone, my sweet child. My death does not mean that I am gone. No, I am with you *always*. If I could have stayed, you know I would be right there *always* holding your hand... guiding you... loving you.' Mel could no longer stand the distance between them. She leapt into her mother's arms, hugging her so fiercely at that moment, sobbing with her knees weak, completely broken.

They stayed like that for a while with Sade holding her, comforting her the way Mel had always craved for years until the last mews coming from Mel came to a slow stop. Sade took her hand and led her to one of the engine-red swing seats and plopped her down firmly. Sade began to push her, and at first, Mel found it so silly, but she started to grin wide like a Cheshire cat. They played and talked like that for a while. Sade told Mel all about her childhood and how difficult it was moving to a new country where she never felt appreciated.

'I loved the thought of education and I wanted to be more than just a wife, you know. What opportunities were there in Nigeria for a woman like me? Your father and I, oh my... we struggled for *years* to scrape up the money to come to Britain. We didn't want you girls to go through what we had to... but it wasn't easy when we finally *did* leave.' They shared looks of understanding and cried together.

After more time passed, Sade took Mel's hand again and silently walked with her for a while, until they came to a fork in the road. Sade reluctantly let go of Mel's hand and went to go stand on the left side. As soon as Sade got there, more luminous figures appeared. They seemed so familiar to Melody and she felt warm just being in their presence. They were all women, dressed in black and blue like her mother, standing in an arched row looking at her, smiling fondly. This was her family; her people. And she was their legacy. Melody knew then that she couldn't stay. No, she *had* to go back; make amends, and do better this time around. Her ears tingled in anticipation, but she was confident in her decision.

'Thank you,' Mel said. Not just to her mother, but to all the women that stood before her.

'Take care of my soulmate for me,' Sade called out to Mel.

Salty tears started pooling at the corner of Mel's eyes. This time, Mel did not want to hurriedly wipe them away. She wanted to feel them roll down her cheeks and not have to hold in her emotions anymore.

She mouthed 'I love you' to her mother as she walked right. She kept walking and walking until that blindingly bright light appeared again, obscuring her vision.

Lying down with her eyes closed on an uncomfortable hospital bed, with her father holding her hand in both of his while saying some silent prayers, a small smile crept onto Melody's face. A tree at last.

Glossary

- Buba: A blouse
- Iro: A large piece of fabric worn wrapped around your lower half; like a skirt. The iro and buba are worn together.
- Aaro re nso mi: I've missed you.

Leaf Storm

i.m. my mother

Dara Kavanagh

Dara Kavanagh is the penname of David Butler. His novel 'City of Dis' (New Island) was shortlisted for the Irish Novel of the Year, 2015. His second short story collection, 'Fugitive', is to be published by Arlen House later this year. His third poetry collection, 'Liffey Sequence', is also to be published in 2021 by Doire Press.

Some days after the diagnosis
set time, a death-watch beetle,
ticking, you set out undaunted
for the park. Your time of year -
air cold as water, the trees
touched with fleeting majesty.
As we rounded a beech copse,
a puckish wind stirred up and,
like Dante's fugitives, drove all
about a streaming leaf storm,
shoal-dense and endless, brass
after brass, chattering, sheering
in great murmurations, showing
the raw grandeur in letting go.

Another Place

Petra Lindnerova

Petra Lindnerova is a student of Contemporary Literature, Culture and Theory at King's College London. As an exophonic writer, she enjoys peeking into the relationship between creative expression and identity. She is a sub-editor of Strandlines, a portal exploring lives on the Strand, and works as a freelance content writer. Her fiction has been published online by Reflex Fiction and in the KCL Literary Society anthology, Inside Your Mind.

The two weeks I wander around my parents' house turn me into an archaeologist. I dive deep into the dark closets and drawers, thrilled with the prospect of opening old boxes and breaking time apart. I work quietly, blowing the dust off books and files, wiping away years of it as I shovel towards the past. I know that this trip is only self-inflicted — I can turn around anytime and renounce the nostalgia.

Among the remains, I find two phones. Each is excavated from a separate realm of the house — the old wooden cupboard under the staircase mother used for storing shoes that didn't fit anyone; and the depths of my bed, between the mattress and the headboard, where I used to hide my guilty little diary. I charge them both to give them a second chance.

The older one is a purple flip phone dating back to high school times, me as a cool kid always running down the corridors in the newest shoes, my soles squeaking as I went. My best friend Mira had a matching phone, complete with an array of stickers down the back. We would buy new ones every week and decorate together, haggling and swapping pieces like gemstones. We rarely argued. Mira was a minimalist; she liked simple flowers and hearts. I, on the other hand, wanted everything as glittery as possible, wanted the phone to be shimmering from a distance as I put it to my ear to pretend somebody was calling me.

It was easy to be proud of one's possessions then. Nobody blamed you if you were a kid. It always gave Mira and I something to do — make it look pretty, send texts to get a horoscope, or just show each other new pictures we downloaded. There was always something to compare.

Now, in all its neglect, the phone looks dull, its colour rubbed out into an unattractive faded pink. It hasn't been held by a giggling teenager for a decade.

I flip it open. The smiles of two young girls light up,

catching me unprepared. I want to smile back at them, but the brightness coming from the screen stuns me.

The phone is full of photos — balls, parties, the concert of our favourite band. My parents drove us to another country for it. They were always my ideas, those trips. She used to say I had the perfect parents. We were so different, yet we went together everywhere.

I pace around the house, stumbling over open boxes in my worn-out slippers, the girly plastic toy in hand. She has been here so many times — we drank my father's Malibu in this very living room. I'd never been drunk before and thought I had a fever; she almost laughed her head off. I never truly miss her, mostly because I feel rejected.

She was obsessed with my dog, who's now buried in the backyard. She called him perfect.

She visited me in London once or twice after I had moved. I wanted her to stay, but she wasn't listening to me and kept taking pictures of everything around. Our favourite band was from there, but when I made a reference to one of their songs, as the bus stumbled through the narrow streets of Peckham, she smiled without recognition. I suddenly wished for her to be gone already so that I could go back to memorializing her. As a parting gift, I gave her stickers of the London band she had already forgotten.

I go outside to sit by my dog's little tombstone and stare at her number. It's huge and pixelated, outdated in every sense.

After a few rings, I hear a breezy voice. 'Hello?'

It hangs in the air like a spectral echo. It could as well be coming from the grave below me. It's the first person I've heard in days.

I clear my throat, unused to the ropes of conversation. 'Hi, Mira.'

She doesn't recognise me. I feel an urge to start whistling

our favourite song, but the band has broken up, so I just think of my dog.

'It's Aria. I am here with Spotty, and I thought of you.' I look towards the sky with an apology addressed somewhere towards dog heaven for using Spotty as an icebreaker. The other side stays quiet.

'Oh!' She exclaims after a while. 'How is he? Rub him behind the spotted ear, will you?'

I look at the shiny cold stone, and my throat tightens with the effort to remember whether the black mark was on the right ear or the left. I fail.

'He's happy.' I say. 'He wanted to know how you were doing.'

'I am alright, given the circumstances. Mostly at home with my family. Are you in London?'

'No.' I press the root of my nose to suppress a sniffle. 'I'm back at my parents' house.'

'That's great! Give them my best, please.'

I nod forcefully. She won't ask. The conversation is polite. She works in accounting. Her dog is still alive. She does not have a boyfriend at the moment, but as she says, that never mattered to her.

I recall how I came to her house late one night and broke down because of Laurie. It makes me hate Laurie and miss Mira.

'We should meet up once this insanity is over,' she suggests. The tone is too deep. I stare at the dates on Spotty's tombstone.

'We definitely should.' I reply. My vision is a blur, but none of it makes its way into my speech.

'I'll get in touch when things calm down.' I hear someone calling her name in the background and wish it was a person I knew. I probably wouldn't recognize a mother's voice anymore. Are they still warm and overbearing?

'Sure.' I stay sitting on the grave, convoluted into a knot of achy limbs. As we hang up, the phone feels heavy in my palm.

Things will never calm down.

For me, leaving used to mean relaxation. I never liked the word escape, giving me the feeling of rushing around with a suitcase, sweat dripping down the armpits, and heavy breathing. Leaving was mental yoga — it helped me sleep. Leaving London to come back to my hometown was supposed to be just another short workout. I should have stretched my legs, done the downward dog and child's pose, and greeted the sun. I wanted to say goodbye.

Instead, I get stuck in position, worried a wrong move would break my bones.

The second phone is quite a leap technologically — there is no need to make any sort of movement for it to come alive. A simple tap is enough. It's always there, ready and waiting to be wanted.

I open a bottle of Merlot to accompany the bitterness induced by the look on Laurie's face and step outside again. He was incredibly photogenic — in the right light, his eyes would turn emerald and make me come off even plainer than usual. This was one of those moments. We took a selfie while having a picnic in the prime of the summer. I wore a black jumpsuit because I wanted to look thinner, and he was wearing his usual whatever and still looked ten times better.

I got the phone around the same time I met him. I remember because it gave me a sense of starting anew. The case was white and clean, and I was over stickers at that point. I felt like an elegant woman sitting with my legs crossed, waiting for him at a bar, texting to let him know I was waiting. I would ask for wine and drink half of it before sending another message.

There was a photo he had taken of me feeding a squirrel. I don't remember the little animal, only him smiling from behind the phone as he zoomed in on me. For a long while, he was all I could see.

He loved me drinking red wine and used to say my lips looked fuller with every sip. I made it my staple drink, taking long swigs in the hope the colour would leave a permanent effect, like a cheap alcoholic version of botox.

He always wanted to be with me, but the time was never right — neither his nor mine. I fed so many squirrels waiting for him to show up.. I made their tummies ache with heaps of nuts while I drowned my liver in wine, sometimes too tipsy to bite my tongue when he finally arrived. He would never argue with me. Instead, he'd fall into silence as perplexing as a death sentence. We would meet again after a few days, the later the better, and have sex. My dreams were invaded by squirrels every night. They nibbled on my hair and pinched my lips until they looked raw.

My parents' garden is wild and overgrown. As I walk the perimeter with a glass in hand, the mud sticking onto the soles of my slippers, I get taller and taller. I keep counting the circles and allow myself a sip after each. Those green eyes are staring at me with their unceasing intensity, and I know I could play with time again.

I've made enough circles for my lips to get swollen. I can feel them dominating my face, almost pursed in anticipation. The number is too fresh in my memory, and I don't feel as excited as I should. I continue with my laps as I dial, my slippers getting heavy with chunks of mud.

'Hi, Aria.' He pronounces my name as a single breathy syllable. He doesn't stress it, but I do. Goosebumps are climbing up my neck.

'Hello. I am back.' I was never particularly good at shocking him, but I can discern a slight gasp this time.

'With your parents?' he wonders.

'At their house. They're not here.' I want to touch my lips to ground myself, but my hands are full. I stare at the bottom of my glass, swinging it and playing with a single red drop to make it loop around. He will ask.

'Where are they?'

'Gone,' I look up, apologizing for another ice breaker.

'You came to an empty house?' I know this tone. It's more opportunity than pity, and that makes it strained.

'Yeah. I'm in the garden now,' I reply as I add up to my score. Every step takes genuine effort now, as if I had weights strapped to my ankles.

'You don't seem okay.' His tone remains the same. Chance over disturbance. I can hear him shifting around, picturing my lips ripe and ready to tell him to come over. His hand is probably floating above a set of car keys at this very moment.

All of a sudden, I can't lift my leg. I'm stuck.

I prepare the last remaining bottle of wine and hop into the shower. My socks are completely damp from crossing through the sludge, leaving messy footprints. I had to leave the slippers in the middle of the garden, sticking out of the ground like two unhappy friends.

I find the jumpsuit at the bottom of the wardrobe, but my hips are now too wide to allow me the luxury of dressing up.

Seeing him is the same every time I am back. Wherever we meet, there is always a light to turn his gaze emerald, and I feel pale and stale. He utters his condolences, then whispers my name in the hope of making me mistake longing for belonging. We drink straight from the bottle, sitting on the leather sofa. He is disappointed to find out there is no more wine. I motion towards the bar where my dad's bottles still stand in formation, and observe as he rummages through it. The room is swaying at this point, so it takes some time for me to focus on the white bottle he holds up as a potential winner.

My face twists in a spasm. 'No. Not Malibu.'

He inspects the bottle, an amused grin flying up and down his face as it floats towards me and back again. I feel too flustered with drunkenness, so I sit up straight.

'I used to drink this ages ago with my mates.'

'Yeah.' I stop trying to look at him.

The squirrels don't come that night, but I can hear them faintly, waiting somewhere in the distance of my conscience. I spring up awake, my lips tasting bruised and the inside of my mouth rough like sandpaper. It's hard to breathe here. The covers are tangled around my legs, and it takes a while for me to uncurl and stand up. I fumble for a source of light to navigate me through the sweat-dense room. The first thing in my grasp is the plastic flip phone.

Laurie's naked chest is rising and falling peacefully. He always sleeps flat on his back. His eyes are slit rather than closed. I have a theory he does it on purpose -- in case he dies in his sleep, he wants to give his eyes a chance to turn emerald in the morning light one last time.

Letting the torch guide me, I pad to the door on my sorry sore feet. I go naked — my clothes were given up to the floor, and I can only see Laurie's shirt thrown over the chair. I can't bear the cliché.

I descend the steps. In the blackness, I expect each of them to swallow me. The phone is a selfish torchlight, only shining around and for itself. I'm embarrassed to be drunk and naked in front of Mira. This feeling is new. I cover my breasts in a silly attempt to stifle my self-consciousness and miss a step.

I land in mud. The phone rolls away, stopping at the wall, propped open sideways.

At first, I want to scream in disgust and get back on my feet. But there are noises other than my surprised heaving. Squirrels, I think, then pronounce myself insane. I stay low, noticing more patches of soil on the floor. Have I done this?

Someone flicks on the light. 'Aria? I thought you were dead!'

The bony pink bundle that I am, I stare at Mira from the floor. She stares at me too — at the screen me. As I hasten to get up, Laurie emerges at the top of the stairs, rubbing the green into his eyes. He's completely awake once he spots me hunched over the handrail, feeling up my bare side. I swear as I touch my lower ribs.

Mira removes her coat and wraps it over me. 'You didn't sound right on the phone.'

I glance to the corner at our picture dimmed by the screen saver. After a couple of attempts to take a deep breath, I excuse myself and go to the bathroom. I wash off the mud, rinsing carefully around my waist. It's too hard to breathe. I can hear them arguing on the far side of the house, their voices raised in agitation — the way they always used to communicate. 'Aria' drops a couple of times. I could rush out and stop them; I could be dramatic.

He says I don't have time for this.

She says you haven't changed then.

He says I was here first.

She says where are her parents?

I feel like my bones are not in the right place. There is a pile of clothes waiting outside the door. I put them on, wincing and panting. Before I leave, I put a thick layer of lip balm on my mouth. I get my wallet and my car keys. I leave everything, and I take no luggage.

Jag Älskar Dig, Auntie

Hanna Järvbäck

Hanna Järvbäck is an international undergraduate student at the University of Brighton studying English Literature and Creative Writing. Born in Sweden, Swedish is her first language. However, since her youth, she found herself moved by the English language. She started writing creatively in English at the age of 15 and often includes a style of hybridity in her writing by mixing languages when discussing culture.

This suitcase of mine
Is far too heavy.
It overflows
With the things she left me.
And not a single thing did I want to miss.
Scattered on the bottom you will find,
Jewellery she kept close and always mixed.
Silvers and golds.
If that is not bravery,
Then I don't know what is.
Jammed in the corner are her glasses,
To help me see.
Because one day she told me,
That despite my eyes are green,
I watch and judge with blue,
And that would make it harder to start anew.
In the middle I have wrapped
The things she told me to care for, gently.
Like the left eye teardrops from her sister,
And the blood from the heartbreak of her mother.
The disorientated mind of her husband,
And the very memory of her soul.
And the suitcase is overloaded,
With all the words,
They all had to say.
Of all the advice she always gave.
To never ropa "hej" förrän du är över ån,
And always kolla till bordet,
När du sparkat med tån.

In this suitcase of mine,
I have put in her shoes,
Although in them I will never walk.
And I cried when I packed her last words,
Jag älskar dig,
And goodbye.

Scattered From The Mountain

Thandi Sebe

German-South African Thandi Sebe grew up in Cape Town. After completing her schooling at the German School in Cape Town she returned to Berlin, the city of birth, where she completed an English BA at the Humboldt University. Since 2015 she has been working as an actor and writer for film and theatre between her two home bases Cape Town and Berlin.

It was almost 35 years to the day that his father had told him that he wanted to be cremated. At the time, H had just started discovering the wonders of masturbation, and so death was the furthest thing from his mind when his father brought up the topic at breakfast between coffee and toast. It took H a moment to understand what his father was talking about, steering – with great effort – his thoughts away from the magazine cover he had caught a glimpse of in a shop window, making sure to save the image in his mind for later use.

Instead of answering his father's request with a 'Yes, daddy' as a good, obedient son would have done, he responded like this:

'Why?'

To which his father replied:

'I want you to scatter my ashes from the top of Table Mountain.'

'Why?'

'Because I've never been up.'

'Why don't you go up now?'

'Because,' his father took a brief but noticeable pause here to indicate that he was about to say something that his son would not like, 'I have to work hard to put food on the table for your greedy stomach, and there is no time to go up there.'

'Ugh,' he uttered - or perhaps a similar teenage sound - but he knew that it was true.

His father continued talking, but H failed miserably at pushing aside the re-emerging images, and so his father's voice drifted somewhere into the ethers of his mind, almost inaudible, until decades later when his father's wish suddenly became important to remember.

For a teenager raised in the 80s, H and his father had a rather open relationship, one where 'talking back', so long as it contained humour or wit, was not punished by lashings, like in some of the other households H had witnessed. In fact, H knew a number of families in his neighbourhood where 'being clever' seemed a sin and was punished quite unimaginatively by a clap with a shoe or a lashing with a branch, or if those were not within reach, with the slap of a bare hand. H had only ever been hit once. He had used a then rather often used word denoting a specific group of people, and he had done so without any malicious intent, but merely to set apart one person from another, in a rather banal situation he was trying to describe. But his cheek stung badly as he looked in shock at his father who seemed equally surprised, as though he was not responsible for the red demarcation of a hand now clearly contouring H's face. After the first moment of shock had worn off, his father whispered into the awkward silence, 'Don't ever try to put yourself above someone else.' And that was all he said before disappearing out of the front door. He did not speak to his son until the following day, when he enquired about who had eaten the last koesister he had so looked forward to. They never spoke about the incident.

Only now, 35 years later, with his father on his death bed – a couch placed in the centre of the living room, from which he had a perfect view of the living room, the kitchen and the flowering hibiscus tree through the window facing the yard – did H suddenly understand the significance of that face slap.

He was busy frying some eggs when his mind revisited the old memory, and suddenly understood the meaning of what had occurred that day. His father had not hurried out of the house because he had been annoyed or angry, but because he had felt two separate instances of shame. One, for having failed to raise a son who was aware of his

place in the world and could utter such a painful word so
easily; and two, because he had failed for the first time in
his life to restrain his own anger. When H's mind returned
to the present moment and to his eggs, he saw that they had
burned to a blistering crust. He threw them into the yard
for the dogs to eat and decided to apologise to his father
for having ever housed that word in his mouth. His father
appreciated the gesture and in turn apologised for having
raised his hand at him that day. All things now settled, and
no regrets or secrets left to share, H thought that perhaps
this meant his father could leave his physical restraints,
plagued by pains, behind and move on peacefully to the
next level. But he lived for another 58 days after that and,
having nothing more revelatory to say, the following weeks
were spent mainly telling jokes or reminiscing about the
nice things that existed in the bad old days. Like summer
holidays enjoyed at over-crowded beaches, trying to stand
knee deep in the shallow end of the ocean without getting
brain freeze.

Then, suddenly, 58 days later, when H had become so
used to his father being on his death bed that it no longer
seemed like a death bed at all, he was gone. H had just
gotten up from the sofa and walked to the kitchen to fetch
his father some more sugar for his cup of Rooibos tea ('One
more spoon of sugar won't kill me!') when he remembered
a joke he had read in the newspaper that day, that he
thought his father might appreciate. He traced his steps
back to the living room to present the joke, only to find his
father gone. Not that his body had physically disappeared,
but H sensed instantly that his father's body was … well,
empty. He wouldn't have been able to describe it other than
in that way; that he looked distinctly 'without a soul'. Gone.
Just like that.

H had thought somehow that it would be more dramatic,

the ending. He had not expected a fade out like in one of those mediocre plays or films where the final scene comes on suddenly and leaves one sitting incredulously, waiting for something more to happen, until the credits roll in and force you to accept that it is over. H had expected more of the ending. And just like a theatre audience that slowly and awkwardly realises that it is now expected to clap, the realisation dawned on H that he too was expected to do something. But he wasn't sure what that was. Surely not clap. Call the doctors? The ambulance? Or sit down next to his father and maybe gently hold his hand in case some part of him was still present and needed comfort during his transition?

He decided to do the latter, and so he sat down beside him on the floor and slid his own hand into his father's, dangling off the couch by his side. H had never realised how large his father's hands were. Much larger than his own. It made him feel like a child, which was most likely also the only other time they had ever held hands like this. Unsure of what to do, he told his father the joke anyway. He realised as he told it that it was not really that funny after all, and so he was hardly surprised after delivering the punchline, that there was no reaction. After a few moments of silence, he placed a kiss gently on his father's head, and then felt with surprise that a tear rolled down his cheek, although he had promised his father not to cry. Not because his father was of the old-school conviction that a man should never make use of his tear ducts, that they served a purely decorative function, but because he believed that there is nothing worth crying about when a man who has lived a good life dies at such an old age.

H made to wipe the tear away quickly, but he was too slow, and it landed on his father's cheek. This made H cry even more because now it looked like his father was crying, and that was a painful sight. When H was finished, he discovered he wasn't sure how long he should sit like this to honour the occasion. The question was answered by a pain in his knee, and he got up slowly, realising that he was also no longer young, and he imagined himself lying there in his father's place, with his own two daughters watching his empty body. He shook his head, called his father's doctor, and then his mother, and then that was that.

And now he was here, walking up bloody Table Mountain in the midday heat, cursing his father for having died in the middle of the hottest summer of the last decade. He wondered whether his father could have imagined that he would live 35 more years after declaring his cremation request, and whether he knew that it would mean H being an old man himself, struggling up a rocky path with two daughters in their pre-teen years, who verbalised their discomfort with every step. Right now, his daughters, not even halfway up the mountain, were hosting a minor strike.

'Daddy, it's too hot, I can't anymore. Can't we scatter them here?' said T, who was by far the naughtier one. And he was tempted to do just that, but he made to honour his father's request and pushed them on.

'We're almost there, come, you're still young.'

Again, T: 'If we make it to the top, you can cremate me too because I will be dead.' And she emphasised 'dead' in that teenager-esque tone; piercing yet bored. H had continued the tradition of his father, that children could 'talk back' so long that it was funny. Although what was considered funny, he acknowledged, differed sometimes according to age group.

'Move!' He pushed her lightly from the back, and she let him push her like that for a minute as they clambered up, out of breath and wondering how it could be that the higher they climbed, the further away the peak appeared. They took another break, although this one was unanimously decided upon.

'Water break!' shouted M, the younger daughter, his baby, and T immediately shifted swiftly towards the only speck of cool stone, shaded by a small shrub.

H didn't sit down, too worried that his knee would not allow for him to raise himself again without his daughters' help, and he knew they would not let an opportunity like that pass without cackling like evil twins about his old and broken body. A young attractive couple, moving with an ease that slightly enraged H, passed them by at that moment, and the woman smiled at his children laying there on the side of the narrow pathway.

'You look like you're having a great' time, she said knowingly to the two tired faces, as she tried not to step onto the backpack that T had dropped in the middle of the path.

'We're going up to scatter my grandpa's ashes. When my daddy was a boy, my grandpa said he wants them scattered from the top and he's not allowed to use the cable car, because he mustn't be lazy,' M had both a skill and a bad habit of opening up to strangers indiscriminatory.

'But my daddy is old and wants us to take breaks every two seconds,' T added to round off the story. At this point H dropped in a word. '

Stop embarrassing me in front of strangers.' The girls giggled at his feigned outrage, and it gave them the energy to continue their arduous hike up, only taking a break a few more times. These were mostly initiated by H pretending to call attention to the sound of a bird, or to take a moment to appreciate a particularly beautiful view. They played along, too exhausted now to make fun of his age, and perhaps becoming somewhat aware of the solemn silence that was spreading across the mountain as they reached the peak, a reminder of the task that lay before them.

When they reached the top and saw the edge of the mountain and the city spread out below like a carpet, H wanted to high five his kids, but he didn't have the energy, and so he remained quiet. His daughters mistook this prolonged silence for solemnity and so they honoured what they believed to be a spiritual moment, and too did not speak. It was the wind that interrupted the stillness, a gush of cold air hitting them from behind suddenly and harshly, like an ungentle lover waking up a sleeping partner with an unfriendly nudge.

'Daddy, it's freezing,' the girls sang in unison, and H quickly, and without a word, pulled from his backpack the two jerseys that he had packed for his girls that morning. They had ignored his cautionary warning that it could get cold on the mountain, insisting instead that 'it's like a million degrees today!'. And of course, such is the life of a father, he had forgotten to pack something warm for himself while packing their bags. While his daughters put on their clothes (neglecting to thank him), H took the box out of the bag and was thankful that he had had the good foresight to pour the ashes from the urn to this light cardboard box.

Gripping tightly to the box, he gently shoved the girls in the direction of where he believed his late father's house was. He cursed the wind, and simultaneously thanked it for propelling him slightly forward with its force. When M came to a halt and said, 'This is perfect!', he agreed. It was perfect. There, below them to the left, lay Lion's Head, draped in fluffy clouds like candy floss, signifying a rainy day to follow this one. The rest of the city was cloudless. There, past Signal Hill, was Robben Island, like a single leaf lost in a large pond. The shoreline that stretched along, housing the wealthiest and the fittest people of this city.

Further to the right was the view of the neighbourhood of his childhood. From up there you could not tell how much it had changed, that the corner store where he used to stand and look at those magazine covers had shut down, making way for a lofty building that seemed to be an office space, café and apartment building at once. Or that the park, once home to a few local drug addicts, and a favoured hang-out spot for him and his friends, had been turned into another mall-like building with not one, but two coffee shops to satisfy the needs of the newly moved in caffeine-addicts. None of that was visible from up here. Just some tiny houses of white walls and red roofs that could be made out by his daughters, and speckles of blurry white and red made out by H, who desperately needed glasses.

'And now?' asked T. H carefully took the lid off the box. He peaked inside. All that remained of his father was this dust, waiting to be returned to the universe.

'Now we scatter his ashes,' he said as he looked around to make sure that they were alone. The cold had cleared the mountain and the few people in the distance were making their way to the Table Mountain shop, presumably to get some coffee. H took a deep breath, smiled at his daughters who had both begun to tear up, and then stretched out his hand holding the box and, slowly and deliberately, with as much devotion as possible, began to pour his father's remains into the wind to be carried into the distance.

But H had miscalculated the wind's direction. He watched in horror as the ashes, instead of gracefully rolling down the edge of the mountain as he had envisaged, were propelled by a sudden gust of wind straight back into H and his daughters. All three of them stood wide-eyed, frozen as the ashes whirled around their faces a couple of times. Then the gust was over, and the ashes settled, some on the ground before them, and some on H's collar and his daughters' hair. They stood silent like that a moment, shocked at how their little ceremony had been hijacked and ridiculed by the South Easterly wind.

Then T said, 'Oh my god!', dragging out the 'o' in 'God' very long, almost like she was pointing out who was responsible for this mess. It was then that H remembered how his father's speech had continued that day 35 years ago. His father had iterated that H should make sure to check the wind's direction before scattering his ashes into the wind. 'But of course, that goes without saying,' he had added.

Now H stood there with his father on his shoes, and he couldn't help but laugh, and once he started, he couldn't stop. His daughters joined in. Laughter turned to crying and back again, until the laughing and crying became indistinguishable. H hugged his daughters, who dug their heads into the comfort of his arms. They stood there for another couple of minutes like that in the cold, with H's arms wrapped around their shoulders, looking into the distance, each one thinking their own thoughts.

Then they turned to make their way to the cableway in silence (permission had been granted to use the cable way on the way down!). H hastily paid for the tickets and they stood in line, which consisted of just the three of them.

'That was a bit more of a bang to the ending,' H thought to himself, and he wished his father could have been there to watch their spectacular mishap, knowing that it would have made him laugh. 'Hope you enjoyed the show,' he said quietly as they made their way back down into the city through the clouds.

Life's Journey

Chloe Tonge

Chloe Tonge is an amateur poet just starting out on her artistic journey. The Covid-19 lockdown has helped her to reconnect with the artist within and begin to share feelings and experiences through words.

The sweet and bitter journey of life
Twisting and turning as it pleases
Through unspeakable joy and toilsome strife
It calmly teaches and relentlessly teases

As fate and faith do often meet
Dancing on the winds of change
To tunes both melancholy and sweet
Lighting the world's largest stage

Beyond the realms of rhyme and reason
Exceeding the reach of mind and heart
Defying the bounds of sense and season
An artist critiques His work of art

Mystery beckoning from around the bend
A discoverer's dream, a sailor's star
Where time and eternity transcend
This restless voyager finds peace at last

Printed in Great Britain
by Amazon

70719379R00102